Part 1

NADI

Keep My Heart,
Until We Meet Again.

A Novel By

JEHANGIR
BADAR

Copyright © Jehangir Badar 2025
All Rights Reserved.

ISBN

Paperback 979-8-89777-670-2

Hardcase 979-8-89906-631-3

This book has been published with all efforts taken to make the material error-free after the consent of the author. However, the author and the publisher do not assume and hereby disclaim any liability to any party for any loss, damage, or disruption caused by errors or omissions, whether such errors or omissions result from negligence, accident, or any other cause.

While every effort has been made to avoid any mistake or omission, this publication is being sold on the condition and understanding that neither the author nor the publishers or printers would be liable in any manner to any person by reason of any mistake or omission in this publication or for any action taken or omitted to be taken or advice rendered or accepted on the basis of this work. For any defect in printing or binding the publishers will be liable only to replace the defective copy by another copy of this work then available.

1

The morning was calm and soft. The weather in March was temperate. Just right. The sun made the sky pink and orange. The air was full of birds singing.

The ground was muddy from the rain last night. The air smelled fresh and new. It was the kind of morning that made you feel hopeful that something good will happen.

I did my chores and got ready for school. Mom was kneading dough between the walls of the courtyard where we always ate. Her hands moved steadily and confidently, as they always did.

"Mom, how long until we eat?" I asked. Not wanting to be late.

She grinned. "First, get some water."

I ran to get it. My heart felt light. That morning was different.

I sat down on the mat next to her.

"Mom?" My voice sounded small. "May I ask you something?"

She smiled and looked at me. "Of course, dear."

I asked "Why do you love me less than I love you?"

She opened her eyes wide. "What? Why do you think that? You are my child. I love you."

"But you love them more." I could barely hear my voice.

Her face relaxed. "They're younger."

"You love the older ones more than me, too."

She looked at me but didn't say anything.

"I know why," I said.

Mom looked at me in shock.

"I know you have other kids," I said. "But I only have one mother. You can show your love. I don't have anyone else to talk to"

She didn't say a word. She might have thought that if she didn't say anything, it would go away. Then Dad came in.

"Get out," he said. That was all he said.

I wanted to stay. I wanted to be with Mom. But I knew better than to argue. This wasn't the first time. I had to leave every time he came. It hurt every time. But today? It hurts more today.

I got up and changed into my uniform. I could see them talking from my window. She seemed delighted with him. So full of life. They didn't see that I was leaving. I had to get to school early today, of all days. After a month, my English teacher finally returned.

I picked up my things and walked past them without eating.

Dad wouldn't ask me if I was hungry. He never did. Mom didn't say anything, though. Did not tell me to eat. Didn't ask me why I was leaving with nothing.

She just let me go.

"One day, I'll leave like this and never come back."

As I walked through the door, the thought hit me hard.

I was the sixth child. We were in the lower middle class. There was no party for my birth. It's just another day. I had a new mouth to feed.

I wanted love when I got older. I wanted to be noticed. But it always went to my dad, my brothers, and sisters. I tried to be different. I attempted to attract their attention. It never worked.

I always thought Mom treated me differently, even when I was a kid. It's cold. Far away. A lot is going on. I became invisible when she was busy. Not useful.

The anger inside me grew slowly and quietly. I stopped wanting love all the time. I wanted to fit in. To be important.

The school was two kilometres away. The path wasn't really a road; it was just a narrow trail that went through fields of crops. Dirt and gravel. Dust followed every step in the dry season. Rain and mud stuck to my feet, making me move more slowly.

The fields on both sides were pretty, but they made things harder. If I make one mistake, I could destroy someone's crops. I had to push through or take strange detours when the plants got tall.

Each day, the walk challenged me. I fall occasionally. My uniform got muddy. I felt the sun beating down on me so hard that I thought I might pass out.

But it also showed me that I could make it through. Each day presents a minor challenge. It provided me with yet another reason to persevere.

I realized something serious as I walked to school on that muddy path.

I didn't love Mom anymore.

She was supposed to love me the most. But she never did. At some point, something inside me broke. I just lost all the love I had for her. It's cold and empty.

I then thought about my English teacher. He was charming. Soft. He made me feel like I was there. He had been absent for a month, and I missed him so deeply it caused pain.

I walked faster, imagining how he smiled and talked. The way he made me feel important.

When I got to school and saw him again, everything felt normal. It was as if he hadn't even noticed I was gone. As if that whole month didn't matter.

I lost the comfort I had felt on the walk. I was so disappointed that I could barely breathe.

I wanted to tell him that I missed him. I had been counting down the days until his return. However, I was too afraid to express those feelings verbally.

The day that started out so well turned into one of the worst days I can remember. It felt like the bright morning was a long time ago. It seemed like everything was dark. I couldn't figure out why the people I loved didn't love me back.

Why didn't anyone care about me?

Years went by without any problems. The years passed from fifteen to twenty-five without any issues. Ten years went by. Some days were enjoyable. Some were very heavy. A lot of the time, I was confused. I felt lost, like I was walking around without a plan.

I kept going anyway.

I kept walking even though I couldn't see what was ahead.

There were days when I was so tired that I wanted to give up. It felt like the road was too long. I felt like I couldn't deal with my problems. I would stop and contemplate those days. Look at how far I had already come. That space gave me strength. It made me remember that I had made it through before. It reminded me that I was capable of reviving my life.

There was one thing that stayed with me through it all. My schooling.

It became my only hope. I continued my education despite feeling that my life was unravelling and experiencing a strong desire to abandon my efforts. It was the one thing that no one could take away from me. It was the one thing that brought me comfort.

It wasn't just tests and books that were part of education. It was progress. It showed me that I didn't have to stay where I was. It helped me plan my days. It kept me going when everything else seemed to be falling apart.

Those years show that I made it through. They were tough. At times, they were mean. But they made me who I am. And through it all, I kept learning. Be quiet. Steady. It was as if a friend were strolling beside me.

I got a job after college. I began to make money on a regular basis. I worked diligently and made my life better little by little. I could obtain better things. I was going forward.

But success brought stress. Stress kept building up. I was always busy. It became clear one day. The job wasn't what I really wanted. I was still looking for something deep down.

That's when I started going on hikes. At first, it was just to calm down. I used it as a way to relax and catch my breath. But it quickly became my safe place.

Mountains. Valleys. Rivers. Falls. They had something that I couldn't discover anywhere else. They made me feel calm in a way I had never felt before.

The scenery was so breathtaking that it appeared as though it was awaiting someone such as myself.

Nature speaks, but not very loudly. You can hear it in the wind, the leaves, the mountains' silence, and the slow flow of water. It leaves marks. It leaves a small path in its wake. It begins in a serene manner.

But just walking through nature isn't enough. You need to take it easy. Look. Hear.

Nature leads you, but it needs you to be patient. Believe. Listen up. It doesn't give you all the answers at once.

I thought that nature was trying to tell me something. It had the answers I was looking for. But I didn't know how to pay attention. I didn't have the time.

I walked through open meadows, over mountains, next to rivers, and on rough paths. For hours at a time. But something strange kept happening. When I finally got to the places I had worked so hard to get to, they didn't feel special anymore. I would stand there and think, "This isn't what I wanted."

Therefore, I looked for something prettier.

I made myself work harder. Pick harder paths. Faraway places. But when I got there, the same feeling came back. No. This isn't it either.

After a while, I figured something out. Beauty is in things we haven't seen yet. The experience loses its allure once we arrive. The magic is gone. What we picture always seems bigger than what we find.

Then there was a time when nothing seemed pretty anymore. The hills no longer held the same beauty. Neither the hills nor the rivers held any beauty. The valleys, brimming with life, hold no significance for me. None of it affected me.

The void inside me got bigger. It went with me everywhere. The world seemed boring. No color. I moved through it like a ghost.

I began to think that the answers were always right in front of me. The answers were on the other side of the river. On top of the mountain. At the start of the spring. I kept saying to myself, "I'll finally understand if I go there."

I went wherever my heart told me to. I believed that each upcoming trip would bring about significant change. But it never did. Any time I was happy, it quickly went away, swallowed by the same emptiness.

The restlessness came back every time I went back to work. I wanted to walk again. The mountains called out to me. They said they would bring peace.

But even there, in the middle of all that beauty, I would still ask myself, "Why am I here?" I was confused. It felt like I was moving without a plan.

Every step taught me something new about the world. The rivers. The wind. The quiet. But no matter how far I went, none of it showed me what I needed.

Things around me started to seem boring. The roads remained the same. The same people. Everything seemed fake. It seemed like what I was looking for was in a different place. Calling me from far away. I could sense it, but I couldn't find it.

Around that time, I was offered a job in a different country. I didn't think twice before accepting it. I had always wanted to go beyond borders. I wanted to discover what lay on the other side. I might find what I was looking for there.

As I packed my bags and left, I remembered something I had told myself before. One day, I'll leave like this and never come back.

And at that moment, I got it. This is it.

I felt heavy and light when the door closed behind me. Sorry, but pleased. I felt like I was leaving behind a part of myself that I didn't need anymore.

2

I went to a different country for the first time. Things seemed different. It felt like I had landed on a different planet. There was nothing I knew. The people, the rules, and the weather were all unfamiliar to me. So far, it's all so different from the life I knew.

Change has always been challenging for me. Adapting to new experiences, particularly unfamiliar ones, was never effortless for me. But once I accepted it and got used to it, it became a part of me. It became an inseparable part of me.

I began making money and living a life that many people would love to have. It looked like success from the outside. It was a steady job. Good pay. I had the opportunity to gain knowledge about a diverse culture. But those weren't the real reasons I came. I was looking for something different. I was searching for something that held greater significance than money or comfort. Perhaps it was a sense of purpose. A feeling of being a part of something. But I couldn't locate it, no matter how diligently I looked.

That feeling of drifting came back over time. I was doing the same things every day, but something didn't feel right. The thrill wore off. The excitement of making money went away. Inside, I felt empty. It seemed like I was living someone else's life. I felt as though I was putting on shoes that didn't fit properly.

Maybe I was still looking for happiness in all the wrong places. The emptiness stayed, even here, where the streets seemed to go on forever, and there were chances everywhere. I found myself pondering whether this journey was merely another stage in an endless pursuit.

This place was lovely. The tall buildings reach the sky and radiate a soft glow in the soft light of the streetlights. There are trees along the sides of wide roads, and the roads are clean and well-kept. There was almost no crime. There was everything. The only problem? You had to pay to get to it all.

But in the bright lights, with the perfect buildings and smooth roads, the question I'd had for years had no answer. The beauty around me couldn't fill the void. The things I bought didn't help. It didn't matter how perfect it looked; it couldn't clean up the mess inside me.

I started to think about the last step I took when I left home. As soon as I said, "This is it." This is the last thing I need to do. Was that really my last step? Were there more people waiting for me to finish? Life is always searching and moving, even when we don't know where we're going.

It was a heavy thought, but it was also strangely comforting. Life wasn't about getting to a certain place. It was about the trip. It was about the actions we take. The things we ask. The void propels us forward. It's possible that the answers weren't in the places I went or the things I bought. Maybe they were in the search itself.

I've never liked quotes that make you feel good. I just did what I thought was right. What made sense was what I did. Life wasn't tidy. Each moment was special and personal. What worked for someone else might not work for me. Life was different for everyone. There wasn't one answer that worked for everyone.

One choice can change the course of your life. People praise you if it works, but they don't contemplate the people who failed on the same path. If it fails, people blame the choice more than the effort or the situation.

There isn't one piece of advice that works for everyone. There is no one way that works for everyone. Every trip is different. Choices, struggles, and experiences shape our journey. There is no set plan for life, and that's what makes it beautiful. It's about getting to know yourself, learning from your successes and failures, and getting stronger through everything. Everyone has their problems to deal with and dreams to chase.

It wasn't straightforward to walk away from what most people spend their whole lives chasing. It was a challenging task. I wanted a life of ease. Safety. But I knew that money and status didn't bring real peace. A title or a paycheck did not demonstrate true peace. It had to come from within.

I felt a strong urge to learn more. I felt a strong desire to deepen my understanding of myself. Mountains, forests, meadows, and streams made my need for them stronger. They brought me back to the basics. So, I chose to go back to my home country. Not because I had failed, but because I wanted to find the parts of myself that I had lost.

A friend, someone I'd gotten to know well over the past few days, told me to check out a nightclub before I left. I had never thought about it before. I hadn't thought about it. He told me it would be a positive experience when he saw that I was unsure. It wouldn't hurt to try it once.

Curiosity won. Even if it was just for one night, I wanted to know.

We got to the hotel and walked through the big front doors. The place was beautiful. Costly and classy. When we walked into the nightclub, it felt like we had entered a different world.

The music was very loud. The lights are bright and colourful. The atmosphere was full of energy. I found a place to sit and got comfortable. At the same time, the atmosphere is both exciting and overwhelming.

Some people sat on the couch and watched and laughed. The dancers moved on stage with energy and accuracy. For a second, I thought I wasn't really there. The dancers moved to the music perfectly. The lights made their clothes shine. Audience members dressed in a range of attire, from suits to jeans and T-shirts, yet all exhibited enthusiasm for the performance.

The air smelled of food from the bar, perfume, cigarettes, and alcohol. As the night went on, the dancers changed a lot. A new group would perform while the others rested. Like a practiced dance, everything went smoothly. Their hearts were on display with every move. Their clothes, makeup, and energy were all just right.

The crowd cheered and clapped. The staff put in a lot of effort to make sure everyone was happy. A young boy approached our table carrying an ashtray, water, popcorn, and a broad smile on his face. Later, we ordered tea while the dancers kept the crowd amazed. I could tell that everyone was really into what they were watching. Occasionally, laughter interrupted the music.

I leaned back and thought about what the night would bring. Not just about the dancers, but also about the world they lived in. The dancers were careful with the crowd. Smiles, hand gestures, and body language. The staff quietly guided the dancers when people were watching. It was teamwork that kept the room alive and buzzing.

I saw a guest walk up to the DJ once. The DJ rushed over and listened closely as the guest talked and looked at the stage. The DJ came back after a short talk, and the music stopped. People in the audience clapped. The dancers stopped and sat down when the DJ said the name of the guest and the dancer he had chosen.

One of the women stood up and started dancing again, but this time she was alone and right in front of him.

At first, I didn't get it, but my friend leaned over to explain. The guest picked the dancer and the song and paid for a private dance. That was the reason the DJ had come to him.

I was curious, so I asked if anyone could do this. My friend nodded. "Yes," he said. "As long as they're willing to pay what the club asks."

At that moment, it hit me. The women worked hard to get people to come because it meant money. The chosen woman's face lit up every time someone asked her to dance alone. One guest went even further. He told a woman to sit down next to him. She walked over, smiled carefully, and sat down next to him. Their hands touched gently. They looked at each other. Don't dance. A short, private, and quiet moment while their song played.

I saw something else. More women came when guests kept asking for songs. Requests were important.

It was my first experience in such an environment, and the atmosphere was sombre. The air was thick with energy that felt almost forced, as if everyone was putting on a show. I got more and more uncomfortable as I watched.

I was about to leave when I saw a woman sitting at the other end of the room. She was unique, calm and elegant. She held a tissue in her hand and tapped her foot to the music. She didn't want to be noticed. She looked far away, like she was watching the chaos instead of being a part of it.

She had a calm look on her face as if she were in her own world. She looked at the stage every now and then, but she stayed away from the crowd. I couldn't take my eyes off of it. I was curious about what made her so unique.

My friend saw that I was uneasy. He suggested that I consider joining other clubs. We went to a few, but they all felt the same. Women are judged only by their looks, and their uniqueness is ignored.

I couldn't get her out of my mind on the way home. That calm presence stayed with me like a soft song. I told my friend that I wanted to go back. He said yes.

The women at the club put in more effort to attract attention. But I only saw one. The woman sitting on the right side. I didn't pay attention to anyone else. The noise didn't bother her; she stayed calm.

She wore a pink shalwar kameez and a matching dupatta over her shoulders. Even though her traditional clothes didn't seem to fit in, she carried herself with grace. She played with the edge of her dupatta and lost herself in her thoughts.

Her beauty was quiet but striking. I couldn't say why, but it spoke to me. The voice inside me that wouldn't stop talking went quiet. It seemed like what I had been looking for was right there.

We looked at each other for a moment. My heart raced. I felt a little better about the emptiness inside me. Finally, the restless voice that had been with me for so long quieted down.

I turned away and told myself that this feeling wasn't real. We looked at each other again. She turned around and took a deep breath. My thoughts were all over the place. Even though I couldn't believe it, a part of me thought she was the one I had been looking for.

How could one person be the answer? That must have been a mistake.

But why did I keep coming back? What made me want to be with her? I couldn't control my conscious mind. My heart and subconscious seemed to know more than my eyes did.

She looked at me now and then, and I caught her looking. Our eyes met for a moment before she looked away. Those quick looks said something—maybe a little interest or a little recognition.

"Is it okay if I talk to her?" I asked my friend.

He looked surprised. "What?"

"Can I talk to that woman?" I quietly asked, pointing.

He smiled knowingly as he looked at her and then at me. "Of course. But she needs to agree first. And if she does, you'll have to pay.

My heart raced. He called a servant at the club. The man nodded and then left. "Upstairs, there's a café. "Go wait there," my friend said.

I stood up to check on her. She watched me move with her eyes. A staff member led me to the café. I was full of doubt. Why did I want to see her? What did I want to say? Chance? Or something more?

Twenty-five minutes went by. Every second felt like it took forever. Thoughts of darkness crept in. What if she said no? Then she came in with the help of a staff member.

My heart raced. She stood next to the chair that was across from me. I got up without thinking, stumbling, and in a hurry. She asked me to sit down with a calm, firm voice.

I sat down. She looked around, taking in every detail with her eyes. There was only one table in the open. There were other tables that were hidden behind walls. The staff brought curtains to give people privacy. She looked at me and waited to see what I would do. I stopped them. I said, "No, we don't need them."

She was beautiful. Elegant and fashionable. Her hair hung down over her shoulders. I noticed a small mole below her lower lip. Her neck, nose, and the curve of her features all displayed perfect balance.

I had seen beauty all over the place, like in the mountains, rivers, forests, and deserts. But she changed how I thought about beauty. It wasn't like anything I'd seen before. It was inside her. People might be the most beautiful things God has made.

I looked at her hands, which were small and still. I watched her eyes as her lashes fluttered. Even a single blink was more graceful than a flower opening up. There was no way to describe her skin tone.

The next morning, on my first flight, dawn came. Seat by the window. First east, then west. The light changed from gold to dark. But none of the other views were as good as hers. She brought back that moment to me: dark but bright, cold but warm.

There was a lot of silence between us. She sat still, looking at me and then away. She had green bangles on her wrist that shone. She moved them slowly, probably to calm them down. She stood there and waited for me to say something. I couldn't think of anything.

There were many different feelings going on: curiosity, doubt, and calm. I kept looking, trying to figure it out.

"Why did you come here, sir?" she asked in a soft, sweet voice that was sweeter than any birdsong.

I was confused when I looked at her. "Why did you come to the club?" she asked again.

I said, "I'm not sure." I don't plan my trips very well. But this is my first time here.

She smiled a little. "Life seems empty when you don't have a reason or goal, right? I don't understand why you wander, but yes, this is your first time here. This applies to any club, as well.

I shook. "I don't understand why I go places." It seems like I'm looking for something, but I don't know what it is.

She turned her head. "Everything has a purpose and a goal. You're not just walking around without a goal." Just because you can't see it doesn't mean it isn't there."

What she said shocked me.

She went on, speaking softly but firmly, "If I had to describe the universe in one word, it would be 'reason.' Stars, rivers, and the wind all have paths." Everything has a reason for being, even if we don't know what it is."

I thought about what she said. Why hadn't I thought of it that way before?

I said, "How did you know this is my first time at a club?"

She seemed calm. "I also know that the man you're with has been here before."

She was correct about my friend. It was strange how aware she was.

I said, "You're right. But how did you know?" Was it a guess?

She smiled, "We don't guess. Stay away from places like these."

"Why?" I asked.

She stared at me for a long time before saying, "There's a reason." I know it, but I won't tell you."

She looked at her phone and stood up straight. "Your time is almost up." I need to go.

I wanted to stop her. But I couldn't get the words out. She was gone.

I sat down and lit a cigarette while I thought.

"Everything has a purpose and a goal."

"Not seeing it doesn't mean it isn't there."

Was my wandering pointless? Or was I just looking for meaning?

My friend came over. "So, you talked to her?"

"Yes," I said, sounding far away.

"Why did you want to talk to her?"

I stopped. "I don't know."

He let out a sigh. "You have to keep yourself in check. No feelings allowed here. Money is the most important thing." Real feelings don't belong."

I said firmly, "She's not fake. She asked me not come again"

He smiled, but he wasn't sure. "She got to you, then."

"Yes," I said.

"Did she tell you not to come back here?"

"Yes."

"That's just how she is." He said, "She's good with people like you."

"Maybe," I said, "But she's not like that."

He moved forward. "Then why did the club staff ask for your number when she went back on stage?" She did it. "Why?"

I stood still and calm. "Why does it matter? This is where it ends. "Let's go."

He followed, worried. "I don't think it's done." This process is just the beginning.

I didn't say anything.

The cool night air outside touched my face, but my mind stayed inside the club, where I couldn't stop thinking about her. I had seen enough. No matter how real she seemed, I knew she couldn't be the answer to my search. My mind was racing, which made it difficult to make decisions.

3

We got back to our apartment at about five in the morning. We weren't in a hurry to sleep because it was Sunday. I left the club, but my mind stayed there. Stuck on her.

I couldn't shake the guilt. Why didn't I tell her so much more? I kept reflecting on her look, her words, and how well she seemed to relate to me. Everything she did, no matter how small, drew me in.

She was beautiful, friendly, and impossible to miss. I couldn't stop deliberating over her, how perfect she was. She was incomparable. Polite, honest, kind, and graceful. She felt almost otherworldly.

I had never felt so at ease before meeting her and talking to her. I felt like all my questions and worries went away just by being close to her. We had a simple but friendly conversation. It gave me a sense of peace I'd never had before.

I felt truly at peace for the first time. I get it. That feeling stayed with her even after she left. It felt like something I had been searching for my entire life without even realizing it.

It seemed like our conversation wasn't finished. The feeling was akin to an unfulfilled longing within my heart. I wanted to see her again. After our meeting, I still had thoughts and feelings that I wanted to share.

It was such a deep experience that I couldn't help but want to locate her and continue where we left off. For the first time, the beauty around me really touched me. This incredible experience seemed to finally fill the hole that had been in my heart for so long.

As I lay in bed, I began to remember her features. Her forehead was clear and open. Eyebrows. Eyes. Her nose, lips, and cheeks accentuated her beauty. That little mole. When I reflected on her, I recognized that I had not truly appreciated her beauty. There was still so much to see and enjoy.

The more I remembered, the more I realized that I had only just begun to understand who she was. Every part of her made me want to explore, and I was completely amazed.

I felt different tonight. Not very heavy. Like a heavy weight had been taken off. I felt less heavy and freer. It felt like I was getting closer to a new kind of happiness.

I fell asleep without even realizing it because I was thinking about her. I slept all day and woke up to find that it was already dusk. My friend had left me missed calls and messages when I looked at my phone.

I got dressed and sent him a message to come over. It seemed like a different day. I woke up and started picking out my best clothes and looking for a good cologne. I had never thought about wearing perfume before. I usually just put on whatever I find. But today, I wanted to look good.

When I got in the car, my friend looked confused. It was Sunday, and I usually would have worn simple clothes, but today I tried.

As he started to drive, he asked where we were going.

I said right away, "The club."

He pulled over and looked at me in shock. I turned around and said again, "We're going to the club." Come on, let's go.

He wasn't pleased, but he got in the car anyway.

I didn't say anything during the ride because I was lost in thought. I had planned to look closely at her face today and remember every little thing about it. I chose to start with her forehead.

There was still time before the club opened. On the way there, we stopped for dinner first. As I walked by the hotel entrance, my heart rate went up. I followed my friend inside. He was ahead of me.

When we got to the club, it was empty. No other guests. There were only empty chairs. The women on stage were talking instead of dancing. We were told to sit in the front row, but we chose seats in the back.

As soon as we sat down, someone came over with popcorn and an ashtray and asked if we wanted tea, coffee, or a drink. I took a close look at the stage. She wasn't there.

I saw her walk gracefully up to the stage a little later. She sat down, crossed her legs, looked at me, and fixed the hem of her shirt. She looked at me every now and then, and I kept looking. She turned away quickly every time I looked at her.

I wanted to be alone with her again. I couldn't wait any longer. I was too eager to hold myself back, so I told my friend, "I want to sit with her at the café again."

"Again today?" He asked, his voice getting more and more annoyed.

I said firmly, "Yes, again."

I could tell he didn't like that I wanted to see her again. He stopped for a moment, then turned to me and said, "Not right now." You will meet her, but not right now. You have to wait until the club closes.

"I can't wait for it," I said. I had to see her right away.

My friend thought about it for a moment before calling the club staff and talking to them for a short time. Finally, a staff member asked, "How long would you like to stay?"

I had a difficult time answering, "How long can she stay?" I asked.

The worker said, "Sir, as long as you want." You pay for the time. If you like, she can stay with you at the café all night.

I said right away, "Okay, all night."

They nodded and said, "Yes, sir." Please go to the café.

My heart raced with excitement as I got up and ran to the café. I was so happy to have more time to really look at her beauty.

The table we had sat at the day before was empty when I got to the café. I went right to it and put my lighter and cigarette on the table. Someone quickly brought over an ashtray. I lit my cigarette, took a long drag, and felt a rush of happiness.

She would stay with me all night.

I thought about what I would say, how I would talk to her, and how I would make the most of this time.

After a short wait, she came. As soon as she got close, I stood up and put out my cigarette in the ashtray. She sat next to me, and her calm, graceful presence filled the room.

Tonight, she looked outstanding in a red suit. Every time she moved, the red bangles on her wrists caught the light. Her hair was loose and silky over her shoulders. Her lips were a soft shade of pink. It was difficult to tell if it was lipstick or natural.

The little mole right below her lips, near the lip line, made her look even better than she already did. I became obsessed with every little thing and started looking.

But it looked like she was more interested in watching everything around her. With quiet interest, her eyes moved around the room. Then she looked at me and asked,

"Sir, why are you here today? Do you have a plan, or are you just here again without one?"

Her words made me think of yesterday when she asked the same thing, and I told her I often go somewhere without thinking.

I paused, unsure of how to respond.

"Today I know why I came. I wanted to see you again and talk to you. I've travelled many paths, but the one I'm on now has given me a comfort that no other path ever could," I said, my voice calm but a little rough.

"He who seeks or finds comfort in paths can never reach the destination." But what do you want to talk about?" she asked, her voice soft but firm, gently pushing me to say more.

I took a cigarette from the table, lit it, and took a slow breath. The smoke curled between us like a veil as I breathed out. I looked her in the eye.

I said in a strong voice that carried the weight of years of wandering, "I know many paths that were more beautiful than the destinations."

She gave me a look that she had never given me before. For the first time, as I had something to say that was worth hearing.

She said, "What do you want to talk about?" in a calm voice.

I looked at her, and our eyes met for a moment. I quickly turned away and took a long drag on my cigarette to calm down.

"Say what comes to mind, sir. Later, you'll walk home and think, 'I should have said this" she said in a soft but firm voice.

I looked at her in awe. What she said shocked me. How did she know exactly what I was thinking last night? She also talked about what would happen to me in the future. What would come next? It was not just about knowing what had happened to me.

I just kept looking at her, caught up in her presence. I couldn't find the words.

Then the orange juice came. I had completely forgotten what I wanted to say or even why I was there. I wanted her to always be in front of me. I wanted to stay in that moment.

She drank her juice and said, "Sir, I asked you this yesterday as well. Why do you come here?"

"Why do people come here?" I asked as I picked up my glass of juice.

She drank with the straw between her lips and her eyes on me. "People come here to charm hearts, satisfy their lust, and use us. They come to see our lovely, naked bodies. That's all this place is for," she said as she set the glass down on the table.

She stopped and asked, "Are you here for the same reason?"

I was surprised and a little embarrassed when I looked at her and said, "Do you think I came here for the same reason?"

She said, "I don't think so. That's why I keep asking. Why are you here?"

I didn't know how to answer her question. I would rather not tell her that; I just wanted to remember the lines on her face.

She then said, "We want people to come here. That's why we're here. Bringing guests is our job. It keeps our house and the club running. This place isn't for someone like you. So, when I ask why you come here or try to talk you out of coming, you stand apart from the others."

She kept talking, but I couldn't stop staring at her forehead. As much as I could, I tried to take in every detail of her face, especially how beautiful it was.

"Why do I come here? Do you really want to know? You might find it weird, but let me tell you something first. Maybe I'm one of the lucky ones who've seen the most beautiful sights in this universe. Nature has created these sights specifically for a select few. Those who wander aimlessly, losing themselves in deserts and mountains, are truly fortunate. I've kept those images locked in my eyes. But even with all that, I've never felt the kind of wonder, joy, and peace I feel now. Since yesterday, this feeling has topped everything else. And what I've seen since then is more beautiful than anything I've ever seen before." I said this without pausing.

She looked at me for a moment, then smiled softly and said, "You can only say that something is the most beautiful so far. Who knows? You might see something even more beautiful one day."

I had to stop and think after she said what she did.

"I doubt that will happen," I said, and as I spoke, my eyes went to the small mole under her pink lips.

With a playful look in her eyes, she asked, "You think so? But can we really think?"

I didn't understand. "What do you mean?"

"We think that we think freely, but that's not true," she said. "Our minds only work with what we've already seen, felt, or lived through. We just shuffle old ideas."

After a moment, she said, "That's why you can't say there's nothing more beautiful than what you've

She smiled and asked me, "Do you know what the final purpose of a person is? What is the one thing that everyone wants?"

I stopped and thought for a moment, not sure right away.

She said again, in a calm but firm voice, "That means you don't know. But you say you've felt it, even though you don't really know what it is?"

The waiter brought us the menu while we were sitting down, but she politely gave it back. When I asked her why she hadn't ordered anything, she said, "I don't eat dinner at night. I'll have breakfast later." She smiled a little.

After that, there was a long silence between us. I kept looking at her face while she sat quietly, lost in her own thoughts. There was something about it that drew me in.

I looked from the faint line on her forehead to the soft curve of her eyebrows. It was like looking at a long road that never ends. It was a sight I could gaze at for days without reaching the end.

She didn't think about the bangles on her wrists; she just played with them, running her fingers over them like she was lost in thought. Every so often, she looked around, taking in everything around us carefully, as if she were trying to figure out what was going on.

She would sometimes look at me closely for a short time before quickly looking down. It was like she didn't know whether she should keep my attention or look away.

"Do you know anything about me? Do you know the life I live?" she asked when she turned to face me this time. She didn't look down.

I didn't say anything; I just stared at her, not sure what to say. She held my gaze, clearly waiting for me to say something.

Finally, I asked, "Do I need to know?"

She said, "I believe you should."

She stopped for a moment, then continued. Her voice was steady, but there was a hint of weakness in it. "I work for money. The person with the most money gets closer to me. Feelings don't matter here. I dance for one person, then another. I have to smile for everyone. I have to perform. In this place, money decides everything, and I do whatever the customers want."

She stopped for a moment and said, "I didn't ask you why you came here because I don't like you. I asked you because of the road you're on. You don't know where it goes, how rough it gets, how dark it gets, or how deep its holes are."

I had to stop and listen because her voice had weight. Kind but firm.

She then looked me straight in the eye and said, "Sir, everything here is just an illusion, and you seem like someone who is looking for something real."

She stopped, as if she were choosing her words carefully. She went on, "We're trained to smile and attract people, to bring in customers. When I first saw you, I thought you were just another guest, another person I could use for business. But then something strange happened. For the first time, my heart told me something different. A voice inside me said, 'Let this one go.' It told me you don't belong here."

She looked down for a second, then back at me, her eyes full of quiet strength.

"I'm breaking the rules of this place by telling you this," she said, her voice getting more serious. "I won't tell you why. Just understand. This is a place for fun, not for people like you. Please don't come back. Even if you do, I won't see you. I can't say no to you, but I will."

She said it all in one breath, as if she had been holding it in for a long time. Finally, let it go.

She was more than just pretty. She was honest, smart, and charming, a complete Woman.

I stopped when she spoke. I took one last drag on my cigarette and threw it in the ashtray. I said, "I'm not going down that path. I came here once, met you briefly, and felt like there was more to say. But your words made me think. For the first time, spending time with someone didn't feel boring. Don't worry, I won't come back."

She seemed shocked. This time, I turned away so she could think about what I had said.

She checked the time. She was supposed to stay until the club closed. I looked at the clock and said, "You can leave if you'd like to."

"I'll leave when it's time," she said. "You paid for this, so it's my job to stay."

I said, "No, really, you can go if you'd like to. You don't have to stay just because of that."

She looked at me and then asked the waiter to bring a coffee.

We sat in silence; with the words we didn't say hanging in the air. I looked at her, but she didn't look back. Not until the coffee came.

Before she drank, she said, "You promised you wouldn't come back."

"Yes, I promised," I said with a smile.

We just looked at each other until the club closed. I was so into the moment that I felt like it was the last time I saw her.

She checked the time and said, "It's time to go."

I stood up and grabbed my phone, just like she did. Before she left, she looked at me for a second.

I sat there, and soon my friend came over to me.

"Why did you really see her today?" my friend asked on the way back.

"I wanted to always remember her face," I said.

"So, did you?" he asked.

I said to him, "I couldn't even see her whole forehead. It felt like it would take months to really see it all."

He looked at me in shock and said, "I think it was a mistake to bring you to the club."

I just smiled.

4

It had been a week since I last saw her, but I still thought about her. Her memory stuck with me like an unwanted guest. When I thought of her, one part of me felt at ease. Another side felt anxious. I was different after that moment. This transformation was evident in my feelings, thoughts, and even in how I perceived myself. It wasn't just about how she looked. She somehow made me feel both calm and empty at the same time. When I was in pain and doubt, she showed me that people can be kind. She made me contemplate what true beauty is. Her face was the first thing that entered my mind when I thought about beauty. I kept contemplating what we talked about. She had left a mark on me that would never go away.

She lived in a world where everything had a price, but what she said felt real. So, who was she to me? Was she supposed to help me, or was she just a mirror showing me what I needed and wanted? Being near her made me feel better. There was a chance that she was somehow linked to the answers I had been looking for. But my conscious mind fought against it. How could the answer to my search be someone who danced to different songs for different people? I was stuck in a storm that made no sense. I can't decide whether to let my feelings in or keep them out. It was challenging to say no to them. But I found peace when

I welcomed them. This was the peace I had been looking for. It made me feel better and less empty.

She stayed in my mind. I didn't go back because I wanted to keep my promise. It had been seven days. I wanted to see her every day and every moment, but I stopped myself. I couldn't take it anymore after seven days. It was too much to wait. It felt like a storm was brewing in my chest, threatening to tear me apart. It felt like my head was going to explode. Every thought and moment brought me back to her. I would break if I didn't get away soon. Even though it hurt and didn't make sense, the pull was too strong to resist.

I started walking toward the club one night almost without meaning to, as if my feet had a mind of their own. This time I was by myself. I hadn't even told my friend that I was going. It could have been shame. Or maybe it was fear. I was afraid that if I said it out loud, I would talk myself out of it. Although it was cold outside at night, my doubt felt just as intense as ever.

I kept telling myself that I wouldn't ask her to the café on the way there. I wouldn't even say anything to her. I would just watch her from a distance. Stay quiet in the club, where it's dark. That would be enough. It had to be enough. Then I remembered that I had promised to leave her alone. It hurt a lot. My mind yelled at me to go back and honor the line I had drawn. But her memory was stronger than any vow. Her grin. The musical sound of her voice stayed with me long after she had spoken. Too clear, too real in my mind.

I couldn't help but want to see her. To be near her, even if only for a short time. It wasn't just a want; it was a need. As important as breathing, such intimacy is a basic need. Even though I felt guilty and the voice told me what would happen, I kept walking. There was a battle between reason and stupidity with every step. I was torn between what I wanted and what I knew was right.

My hands were shaking by the time I got to the club. My mind was all over the place. It felt like I stood outside for a long time. I was stuck between the decision to go inside and the urge to turn back. What if she saw me? What would she say? What if this one weak moment ruined everything? But the guilt of never knowing or trying was worse.

I took a deep breath and pushed the door open into the dark room. My heart was racing like a drum in my chest. I was so scared and excited that my whole-body shook. It felt like my heart was going to jump out of my chest. There was a strong smell of sweat and perfume in the air. The loud music and bright lights hurt my senses. There were many fake smiles and forced laughter in the room. It felt so different from the storm that was raging inside me.

I sat in the back, next to the wall. I yearned to conceal myself and remain unseen. But my heart wouldn't stop racing even in the dark. It raced like it knew something my brain wasn't ready for. I would rather not see the stage. I was afraid of something strange that got worse every second. I kept my eyes down, looking at the empty cups, the flashing lights, and the people who were lost in their worlds. I tried to calm down and breathe, but my hopes were suffocating me.

But eventually, my curiosity won out over my caution. Slowly, I raised my eyes to the stage. Almost without wanting to. She was sitting alone, away from the group. Her presence was too much. When our eyes met, I knew she had been watching me. A shock went through my chest. Sharp and paralyzing.

But her face didn't look friendly. Her eyes were sharp. Even mad. It was like they were silently yelling, "You shouldn't be here." There was no warmth or sign of welcome. It was just a cold, purposeful distance that hurt more than words could.

I couldn't take my eyes off of her, even though she was clearly upset. It felt like her stare was holding me in place. She made me take responsibility for what I had done. But she broke the link first. She moved her head quickly and with purpose, as if it were the last time she would do so. It was a quiet no. It was a clear sign that I wasn't welcome. It left a painful reminder of the line I had crossed.

But even though my chest hurt, I couldn't bring myself to leave. I was stuck between need and guilt, wondering if I had made a mistake. Or maybe I had known all along that this was where I was meant to be.

She kept herself busy by playing with the bangles on her wrists. I couldn't help but notice the small mole under her lower lip that caught the light and stood out. There was a lot going on in the club around me. The walls shook from the loud music. The people in the crowd were really into the live show on stage. The thrill of the evening engulfed everyone. But none of it was important. I was completely focused on her.

I sat there with the club noise all around me and the silent storm in my head. The bass of the song shook my chest and pounded through the floor. The chaos inside me felt even bigger. I fought to make sense of the feelings that were rushing through me, each one pulling me in a different direction.

What was it about her that made me want to hold on to her? Why did she mean so much to my happiness and my path? I didn't get it. It wasn't just how attractive or present she was. It was something more profound. There was an inexplicable depth to her presence. She was a mystery I couldn't figure out. A song I couldn't finish. But I couldn't look away.

I wanted to write her a love song. A song that would bring us closer together, even if only for a short time. A song that would say everything I couldn't say. But I didn't want her to be called up to dance on stage. That wasn't the point. This was only for her. This was not intended for the show or the crowd. But I didn't know how to make it happen.

It felt strange to even think about calling the DJ over, who was lost in his own world of music and rhythms. At first, I was too scared to signal the DJ to my seat. I raised my hand with my heart racing. He saw me and walked through the crowd.

I leaned in close when he got to me. My voice barely cut through the music. "Could you play a song for me?" My throat was tight with nerves.

He nodded, and I slowly pointed her way.

The DJ looked where I pointed and then turned his attention to her. He smiled and had a knowing look in his eyes.

"The one wearing the blue shirt?"

I said "yes" quickly, my heart racing so fast I thought he could hear it.

"Could you do this without bringing her on stage? Only for her. She stays sitting."

He stopped for a second, then nodded to show he understood.

"Got it."

The music stopped all of a sudden. The DJ's voice was loud and clear in the club.

"This song is for Miss Nadia."

I said her name three times under my breath.

"Nadia... Nadia... Nadia..."

I thought that saying her name could help me get to know her better. I couldn't figure out what her name meant. I whispered, "I can feel the weight of it."

"Nadia, a hope."

There was so much in her name. Dreams that aren't spoken. Questions that don't have answers. Things I couldn't fully understand.

I looked back at her when I heard her name in the club. She raised her head and looked around. For something. Or a person. I saw her begin to stand up as if her name had summoned her when our eyes met. But the DJ's voice came back in, strong and clear.

"No dancing."

She stopped and then turned back to me. This time, she gazed for a longer duration. There was something else in her eyes. I couldn't read it. Wanting to know more. A surprise. Possibly something else. I didn't know, but her intense stare made me shiver.

I saw the other women look at her and then at me. Their faces showed that they were interested and maybe even disliked what they saw. It was as if my small act had put a quiet spotlight on us both and changed the mood in the room. The air was thick. Full of unspoken tension.

I sat back down, my heart still racing. I wondered if I had gone too far. Or if I had finally taken a step toward something real.

The last notes of the song faded away, leaving only the low hum of the club. I kept my eyes on her. I was waiting for something. A look. A nod. Even the smallest sign was significant. But she didn't move. She didn't look at me. No smile. Did not say thank you.

It was strange. Not like anything else I'd seen. After their songs, the other women usually nodded or waved. I told myself at first that it didn't matter. I didn't do it to get thanks. But as the silence went on, I started to feel awful in my chest.

I had broken a promise. To stay away. To give her the space she needed. I couldn't shake the feeling that I had crossed a line I shouldn't have while I was sitting there in the dark.

The DJ played other songs after that. The music got louder and livelier. The crowd followed, and their energy grew. But none of it got to me.

Time went by without any meaning. We were sitting across from each other. It was difficult to read her face. At times, she seemed calm and even happy. Other times, I noticed something different. It was as if she was silently asking me why I had come back after she told me not to.

I stayed even though things were tense. I didn't look her in the eye because I didn't want to deal with her anger. Or her unhappiness. I wanted to keep that moment, even though it felt weak.

She looked at me from time to time. Quick glances before looking away. Those times felt like little treasures. There are still thin threads that connect me to her.

Then the DJ's voice broke the silence between us.

"Miss Nadia, please come up on stage."

She gave me one last look. It was hard to tell what she was thinking. Her thoughts were a mixture of emotions that I couldn't pinpoint. Sadness. Acceptance. Maybe a quiet plea for understanding.

Before I could figure it out, she pulled herself together and walked to the stage. That quick look was the last time we saw each other that night. It stuck with me like an unfinished thought.

I noticed something as the music started and she started dancing for a guest. Her smile didn't reach her eyes. It looked like it was empty. Forced. A mask for the people. I couldn't ignore the sharp pain in my chest.

She didn't look at me at all anymore. She focused all of her attention on the person who was paying for it.

I couldn't do anything but watch her dance for him. She moved smoothly, as if she had done it before. The smile I had hoped to see for me now seemed fake. For him. Not for me. It made me realize how far apart we really were. A distance that I couldn't close.

I stayed in my seat as the night went on. I feel guilty and want something terribly. I had come hoping for something.

A sign. A second. But all I found was the truth about her life and where I fit into it.

I slowly began to feel like I was fading into the background. Just another person in the crowd. A short time in her life. The peace I had felt before was gone. An emptiness took its place. A deep ache that made me feel empty. Like something important had been taken from them.

I couldn't go anywhere. I couldn't say anything. I just saw her dance for other people. Her movements were still graceful, but they were far away. Not for me.

She never looked my way. Her smile never got any softer. It was as if I weren't there at all. It felt like I was a ghost. A shadow in the corner. Not visible.

The music thumped all around me. The crowd cheered. The club was full of life. But none of it got to me. I was stuck in my stillness and couldn't move.

I considered leaving. About leaving and not looking back. But something made me stay in that seat. Maybe a little hope that she would look at me again. Maybe fear. Or maybe it was just difficult to let go. To agree that this was all there would ever be.

I stayed, though. Seeing her dance. Smile. Share parts of herself with others. And with each passing second, I felt more and more empty. It served as a silent reminder of what I was unable to achieve. It also reminded me of what I had already lost.

At that point, I knew I had to go. It was too much. Not light enough to carry. I quickly paid my bill and got up. I walked straight to the door without stopping to look back. I wasn't sure if she noticed. Or if she was interested.

At that point, it didn't matter.

It was like a rude awakening to step outside in the cool night air. What I had wanted from her was no longer possible.

I walked down the road without knowing where I was going. I couldn't think clearly. The pavement under my feet, the tall buildings, and the people who walked by me like they were dead. It felt like everything was frozen. I kept walking, trying to figure out what I was feeling.

Then a thought came to me.

Why do I feel so bad?

Why does this hurt so much?

I kept going over everything in my head, trying to figure out why seeing her dance had hurt me so much. I had only met her twice. There was nothing I had promised her. I hadn't even made any promises to myself, apart from not to go back. So why did it feel like I had lost something that I could never get back?

The truth was simple and hurtful. Having her around made me feel better. Her words made me think. She thought she was more than just a person. She gave me hope. She provided me with a glimpse of what I had been searching for. A link. A feeling of purpose. This gave me a reason to believe that the emptiness within me could be filled.

The world seemed quieter when I was close to her. More gentle. Just being there could make the noise in my head go away. But that hope was broken tonight. I realized something I would rather not face when I saw her dance for someone else. Her smile was empty, and her eyes were far away.

She wasn't supposed to be on my path.

She could never be my rock.

My friend.

My peace.

And that truth hurt more than I thought it would.

The peace I thought I would have with her turned into sadness. I felt regret when I realized I had given too much of myself to someone who could never really be mine. It wasn't her fault. It was mine. I had made her seem better than she was. Changed her into something she wasn't. I had to deal with the weight of my hopes and dreams.

I was worn out and let down when I got home. There are no clear answers in my head. A part of me thought she was important to my life. But that weak hope had fallen apart tonight.

The silence in my apartment made me feel heavy. The emptiness inside got louder. More powerful. What if she wasn't the hope I thought she was? The fear of being lost again, without a purpose or direction, came back. I could feel myself slipping back into the same void I had fought so hard to get out of.

I couldn't stop contemplating her even when I tried. No matter how many times I told myself she didn't belong in my life, she wouldn't go away.

Questions kept coming up.

Why do I keep musing over her?

Why can't I move on?

Most important was whether it was possessiveness? Or did I start to own her?

Why I felt so bad and sad, when she danced for any guest?

There were no answers. Just more doubt.

I could hear her words in my head.

"Don't go to the club."

They got heavier every time they played. More important. They weren't just words anymore. They were a sign. A request. I had crossed a line. And now they were with me all the time, loud and clear.

But it wasn't just what she said. It was the memory of her face. The way her face changed when she was asked to perform. There was something in her eyes. A flash of worry.

A hint of something real. It was not the mask that made her appear calm. It stayed with me for a long time after the night was over.

It bothered me. Did she see something I didn't? Or was it all a show to hide how she really felt? The thought wouldn't leave me alone, no matter what.

What was she so worried about?

I kept wondering if she knew how I felt. If she could see how difficult it was for me to sit there, invisible and powerless, watching her smile at someone else.

She had told me.

"Don't come to the club."

I didn't know why until now. I had let my emotions get the best of me. I hoped that she represented something meaningful. I hadn't thought about what she was trying to say to me.

I played back the part where the DJ said her name. At first, she seemed calm. Not quite peaceful. Then things changed. A shadow passed over her face. As if she knew what was going to happen. It was real, but not obvious. A calm unease. It was a silent fear.

Did she know it would hurt ahead of time?

Did she feel the pain before I did?

It all made sense when I looked back. Her warning. She felt uneasy during the show. There was a reason she hadn't spoken. Maybe she knew me better than I knew myself.

Maybe she had been honest from the beginning, in her own way. She was trying to keep me from experiencing pain that I couldn't yet see. She stayed away not because she didn't care, but because she did.

And I didn't pay attention.

I finally fell asleep with these thoughts going around in my head. It wasn't peaceful. Only dreams that were restless and full of pieces of the night. Her face. What she said. The way her eyes met mine for a second and then turned away.

The next morning was heavy and difficult to understand. I woke up feeling confused, with the weight of the night still on my mind. The emptiness was still there. It felt sharper, if anything.

I sat there looking at the wall, trying to figure it all out. Was I wrong about her? What about us? Or did I get it wrong about what I needed? About who I was?

There were no answers. There was only a quiet ache that felt like regret.

The sunlight coming through the window woke me up from a restless sleep later that morning. I still felt sleepy when I reached for my phone. The night before felt like a shadow. That's when I saw it.

A WhatsApp message from a number you don't know.

"Hi, this is Nadia."

I looked at the screen and read it over and over, half expecting it to go away. I didn't answer, even though my heart was racing. I couldn't. Fear? Not sure. I couldn't move because of the weight of everything that had happened.

I tried to forget about her. As I got ready for work, I tried to stay grounded by focusing on simple tasks. But regardless of what I did, she stayed with me. She remained a constant presence in my life.

I kept looking at my phone, hoping for another message. A reason.But nothing happened. That one message was like a question I didn't know how to answer.

The more I looked, the more disappointed I got.

Why didn't she write back?

Why didn't she give it a shot?

It was like a door opened just enough for me to see something I really wanted, but it slammed shut before I could get through. The uncertainty made me restless and uneasy.

I looked at my phone again after work in the evening. There are still no new messages. A storm inside me that I couldn't calm changed from anger to desire. Should I say something? The idea wouldn't leave me alone. It flew around in my head like a bird that was stuck. I finally gave in and sent a brief message.

"Hey"

As soon as I hit send, I started to doubt. Was this a mistake? Would she even answer? Had I only made the situation worse? I kept my phone close by and looked at it over and over. Every time it buzzed, my heart raced. But it was never her. Notifications appear out of the blue. Everything, except for the one I was waiting for, was a surprise.

Every sound gave me hope. This could be her.

But every time I looked, I was let down. It's not her.

The wait became too much to bear. A dull ache is getting worse by the minute. I felt stuck and couldn't move forward. I didn't know how long this feeling would last or if it would ever go away.

Doubt grew stronger as I waited. There was one thought that stood out, clear and sharp.

I shouldn't have answered.

Regret hit me like a cold, heavy wave. It would have been better to leave things the way they were. At least then I wouldn't have to keep going through this cycle of hope and disappointment. It was easier to be quiet than to keep wondering. It was a never-ending cycle of waiting.

I looked at my screen and realized that not knowing was its own kind of hurt. I wouldn't feel this way if I hadn't answered. I wouldn't be sitting here, stuck between hope and nothingness.

I was confused. I wanted to pull away to protect myself from the pain I knew she could cause. But another person of mine wanted to hear from her. To feel that connection again, even if it was only for a short time. I didn't feel like I had a choice anymore. It felt like I had to wait. I felt like I had no power.

I waited, then. My phone is tight in my hand. My heart was torn between hope and fear. I wondered if she would ever answer and what her response would mean.

Why would she even bother to reach out? I couldn't stop thinking about that question. Why now, after all this time? Why send that message if she didn't mean to keep going? Or would she want me to leave her life? Why break the silence just to leave me hanging?

The questions kept going around and around, leaving me confused. But there was one thing about her that stood out. She had never lied before. She didn't play. She didn't give false hope. She never acted like she was. She could have kept me going by giving me just enough hope. But she didn't. She took the harder road. The truth, no matter what happens.

The more I thought about it, the more I wanted to know what set her apart. Why did she care enough to tell me the truth? Why did her honesty not make things clearer? Her truth hurt a lot. It took away my illusions and left me open.

A soft beep brought me back to reality.

I looked at my phone, expecting to see another random alert. But this time it was different.

She had answered.

"Good evening. How are you?"

I looked at the screen. Surprise, doubt, and uncertainty all mixed together. Should I say something? And if I did, what should I say? For a long time, my fingers hovered over the screen before I finally typed.

"Good evening." "I'm fine."

I still felt uneasy after I sent it. Her response had broken the small peace I had found and brought me back to the feelings I had been trying to avoid.

Then a new message came up. Short, but heavy.

"You said you wouldn't come back."

Not long after, another one came.

"This is why I was trying to stop you." I know you and how the world is. This is where I live. You were different in it.

Another message came before I could fully understand it.

"I knew this would happen." I knew how you would react. That's why I told you not to come.

Her words hit me hard because they were heartbreaking and true. She knew it would happen. I fought to keep my distance. She knew exactly where this would end up. Not anywhere. Just nothingness.

I sat there staring at the screen while her words burned into my mind. She had tried to shield me from the truth about her life and the pain that came with it. But I didn't pay attention. I was too focused on my feelings and the hope she gave me to really hear what she was saying.

We are here now. Her messages showed me everything I had been ignoring. From the beginning, she had been honest. I had been too stubborn and too hopeful to accept it.

I wanted to answer. To say something. Anything. But the words wouldn't come out. How can I put it into words? Could I express that I was truly sorry? That I finally got it? It didn't seem like it mattered anymore.

I didn't say anything. What she said affected me. She was right. I was wrong. Knowing that didn't help at all.

But there was still one question. What was she saying this for? Was she just explaining herself, or was there something else going on? It seemed like her messages were more than just an explanation. They seemed like a warning. A request. Maybe even a farewell.

Then another message came, and it was heavier than the others.

"I told you that everything here has a price." Everything is up for sale. A smile or look is fake, even if it's simple. "Life is a masquerade for me."

Her words were very honest. Truthful. They didn't mean to hurt me. They were supposed to show me the truth, even if it hurt.

"I broke my own rules by telling you about this life." I didn't want anyone to hurt you. I didn't want to be the one who made you hurt.

That message seemed real. She was revealing a facet of herself that she typically kept private. A life based on lies and power. It felt like a confession wrapped in love.

There was another message; this one was firm yet apologetic.

"What happened yesterday was not planned. I didn't want it and couldn't stop it. I have no power here. I only go to the shows." I don't have a choice."

There was a break. Then there was another message.

"But I know it hurt you. I feel like I owe you an apology, even though I'm not really to blame. I'll say it now. "I'm sorry."

And then came the words that hurt the most.

"I'm telling you not to come back." Get out of here and don't come back. Live your life as it happens. This world isn't meant for people like you. There is nothing in it. The pain you felt yesterday will only get worse if you stay.

I read her words slowly, feeling how heavy each one was. She was delivering the truth, even if it meant letting me go.

It seemed like she had already made up her mind about how this would end, but I was still having trouble accepting it.

Then a different message came, softer but just as strong.

"You're not the same. Not like anyone else I've met."

I stared at the screen, feeling like there was more. After a short pause, the last message came.

"People like me can't love anyone. We can't be honest with anyone." Not in the life we can live."

Those words hurt, not because she was trying to get away from me, but because they showed how strongly she believed them. She had convinced herself that she didn't deserve love or honesty.

It wasn't only about me. It was her. She had agreed to a life where feelings were risky. Where being real was a risk she couldn't take. And she wanted me to agree with that, too. To leave before the pain got worse.

But I couldn't stop thinking about her messages as I read them. Was she really unable to love? Or did someone just teach her to think that way?

She was doing everything she could to get me to leave. Every word felt like another brick in the wall she was putting up between us. But oddly enough, the more she tried to put space between us, the closer I felt to her.

Her honesty, her warnings, and even her refusal drew me in. And I still can't explain why I couldn't leave.

It wasn't just that she was there. What kept me going was how she saw me, which was different from how anyone else had. I learned things about myself that I had never fully understood by listening to her. She could perceive aspects of me that no one else could. Her insight was truly remarkable. She didn't act like I was just another person in her life. She thought I was real. Someone who deserves honesty and care.

Her honest, unfiltered words moved me deeply. They held a truth that I had never felt before. She looked at me. Not just looked at me. And that connection drew me in, even though I knew it would only end in heartbreak. Real, but strange.

But it wasn't just what she said. It was the way she showed it. She demonstrated it in subtle ways. When it's quiet. The way she listened was truly remarkable. I felt something real there. People don't pay that much attention just to be polite. It came from a deeper place. She was the first person to really pay attention to me. She saw me not as just another face, but as an individual.

After that, she stopped sending messages. That easily.

The quiet was heavy. It was almost too much. I looked at the screen and didn't know what to do. Should I answer? And if I did, what would I even say?

My mind was racing. Should I say how much her words affected me? Should I tell her that what she said moved me?

Should I pretend that her words had no impact on me? I was fine, so I acted like her warnings didn't matter.

I buried my feelings in the end. I answered in a calm, distant way. I hid the truth behind words that sounded calm and unaffected.

But something didn't feel right even as I typed them. It felt like I was lying to both of us.

When she answered, it was precisely what I needed.

"Sir, please don't lie to yourself."

Those words hit me harder than I thought they would. She could see right through me. At that moment, I got it. She was correct. I had been dishonest.

I still tried to stand my ground.

"No, I'm not lying. Why would I?" I answered quickly.

But as I sent it, I started to have doubts. I didn't really believe what I said. It was harder for her to admit the truth than to pretend everything was fine.

Her honesty was like a mirror that showed me things about myself that I didn't want to see. I wanted to look away, but I couldn't. She knew me better than I knew myself.

I wanted to see her again, but asking her was scary. What if she said no? What if this was a mistake? The questions kept going around in my head. But there was a quiet need that I couldn't ignore. After a long wait, I finally typed.

"Can we get together? "I promise, just once."

I held my breath and watched the screen. It felt like minutes passed. Then she answered.

"Okay. Where are you right now? How long will it take?"

I said, "About thirty minutes," without thinking.

"Okay," she said. After a short break, another message came in.

"Come over." Before we go to the club tonight, we'll have coffee. "Same place."

My heart skipped a beat. I answered right away.

"Okay, I'm coming."

At that moment, the pain and emptiness from the night before went away. It didn't matter what else happened; all that mattered was seeing her again. Talking to her. Trying to figure everything out. A calm happiness came over me. I quickly got ready and went to the café.

My mind raced as I walked. It was a different day today. I couldn't stop thinking about where we were going as we stepped into something deeper. I hoped that this would be the last time. I hoped that I could return to my normal life after this. However, another part of me feared the opposite outcome. That this meeting would take me deeper into a world I wasn't ready for.

There was a lot of noise on the streets, but I didn't pay much attention. I couldn't stop thinking about her.

"On what?" she might say. I was fascinated by her potential appearance. The idea that this meeting could change everything made my heart race.

I thought it was a turning point. It felt like a moment that would shape the future of our relationship. My heart raced with excitement and fear as I saw the café.

It seemed like the walk took longer than usual. My mind was racing ahead of me, tangled and restless. I was excited, scared, and drawn to her in a way I couldn't explain. What kind of meeting would this be? Would she stay away? Would she still be honest with me? Would I be able to find the right words, or would they let me down again?

I told myself that this would be the last time. One last talk to get my head straight. To set myself free. But a soft voice inside me made me doubt that. Was this really the end? Or was something going to change again?

I got there five minutes early. The table we had been sitting at was empty and waiting. I quickly sat down to try to calm down. I was shaking when I looked at my phone.

It made a buzzing sound.

"Where are you?"

I typed, "reached."

"Okay."

That one word felt heavy. I stared at the screen, and my heart raced. There was a lot of noise in the café, but I kept my eyes on the door.

Minutes dragged on. My mind went in circles. What would she say? What would she do? Would this help clear things up or make them worse?

Then I saw someone coming. At first, I didn't even notice it. But as she got closer, there was no doubt who she was.

It was her.

I stood up without thinking. She said hi to me in a soft voice that was calm and familiar. She sat across from me, and I sat back with my hands awkwardly on the table. The space between us felt tense, like there were things we needed to say.

Today, she looked different. She didn't have much makeup. What was left was simple and natural. It took me a little while to get used to it. She looked like a different person.

My eyes saw the little mole under her lower lip.

She played with her bangles, and the soft sound they made broke the silence. I grabbed a cigarette without even thinking. Her eyes moved as I tried to light it. First to me. Then to the ashtray, which had three old cigarette butts in it.

She didn't say a word. But the message was clear.

I stopped for a moment, then put the cigarette out. She kept playing with her bracelets. The sound was calming. The world outside the café seemed to fade away.

I wanted that moment to last.

I felt both calm and uneasy when she was there. I couldn't figure her out. A song I couldn't finish. I wanted to remember everything. Every look and move seemed important.

At last, I spoke up.

"I've been on the tracks for years, trying to do everything, but nothing seems important. There is nothing that fills the void. I think you might know things I don't, like you get me."

She smiled softly and looked me in the eye.

"I would help if I could."

The words came out of me.

"Why do I feel this way? why don't I like anything? am I losing my mind?"

She looked at me for a second.

"Maybe it's because something deeper lives inside you, something that makes the world outside seem small."

She stopped for a moment to let it sink in.

"Maybe you're not fading. Maybe you're waiting for something that really fits who you are."

I wanted to tell her she was that thing. But the words were still stuck.

she spoke again, "You are different, you made the world you live in, one full of love and goodness but that world isn't how you want it to be."

What she said hit home.

She looked soft and humble as she sat still with her eyes down. Almost breakable. But her voice was strong and clear when she spoke. There were two sides to her, and I was drawn to both.

"I think you understand me well," I said in a low voice. "It's like you can see right through me."

She turned her head.

"Do you have any other questions?"

I thought about it.

I said, "Not a question." "Maybe our souls met long before we were born." That's probably why you get me.

She smiled softly.

"All right. I have to leave."

She stood up and walked away just like that.

I stayed there by myself. I lit a cigarette after a while. The smoke went up, but it didn't help me relax.

How did she know me so well?

The question stayed in my mind, unanswered.

5

I chose to bury the memories of the last ten to fifteen days deep inside me. It was as if those memories had never occurred. I threw myself into work and had things to do. Anything to keep my mind busy. I told myself that I had found everything I could. No puzzles to figure out. No answers to look for.

No matter how hard I tried, she stayed with me. Like a shadow. Not loud, but hard to miss. No amount of work could make her go away.

No matter how hard I tried to forget, my mind always went back to her. I felt like I was out of control. It felt like an unseen force was pulling me toward her. She stayed on the edges of my mind, waiting for a moment of silence to come back.

I still kept my promise. I didn't go back. I did what she asked, even though I couldn't stop thinking about how much I wanted to see her. I kept telling myself that there was only one thing I could do. What was right?

I always wondered if she was thinking of me when she remembered things. The thought made me feel both good and bad at the same time. Maybe I wasn't the only one going through this if she was having a hard time, too.

I got rid of her number. I would rather not have any chance of getting in touch again. It felt like holding onto a fragile thread that could easily pull me back into something I was trying to get away from. I believed that deleting it would break our connection.

But a tiny part of me hoped she hadn't deleted mine. That hope stayed with me no matter how hard I tried to move on. One day, she might send me a message. Maybe.

I heard the sound of a message notification at the office one afternoon. I felt my heart race as I picked up my phone. It was something I did all the time. I hoped it was her every time my phone rang.

No, it wasn't.

It was my buddy. The person who took me to the club that night. It was night when it all began.

"When are you going to come over?" I have something to tell you.

I looked at the screen for a second, then answered without thinking.

"What is that?"

"I'll tell you tonight."

"Okay," I replied, not thinking much of it. It was like a normal talk. Nothing needs to be done right away. I put it out of my mind and went back to work, not knowing that the night would be different.

He reminded me about meeting up later when I was on my way home. He wanted me to go to his house, but I asked him to meet me somewhere quiet and open instead.

In the end, we walked down a long, empty road. The moonlight softly lit up the area. The street was so quiet that everything felt calm, almost like it wasn't real. We found a bench, sat down, and ate the food we had picked up on the way.

Even while we were eating, I kept thinking about what he wanted to say. He remained silent and appeared to be deep in thought. The quiet made me want to know more.

Finally, he spoke after taking a long drag on his cigarette. His voice was calm, but it was also probing.

"So, you went back to the club."

I was shocked, but I didn't hide it.

"Yes," I said, looking at him. "How do you know? Did you follow me?"

He shook his head and smiled. "Of course not." I know some people there.

I took another drag off my cigarette and got frustrated.

"Say it," I said. "What do you want me to know?"

He paused to take a breath before answering.

"Nadia is smart. She knows how to get people to do what she wants. She messes with people's minds. That's how she does things."

As soon as he said her name, I lost my cool.

"But she asked me not to come back," I said. "She stressed that the second time would be the last."

He shook his head and laughed softly.

"That's exactly right. She knows how to get inside your head. She knows how to read people. You in particular. She won't ask directly for what she wants. First, she'll make you trust her. Then, when the time is right, she will use you. Your cash. Your feelings. And you won't even know it's happening."

He stopped for a moment, then said more firmly, "Stay away." Being attached won't end well.

I made a small smile, but what he said was heavy.

"Use me? How?" I asked. "What do you mean?"

He let out a sigh.

"People like her know exactly what they're doing." They will take anything they can get. And the worst part is that you don't see it until it's too late. Don't get involved, whether it's money or feelings. "This is risky."

I sat there and heard his words over and over. He looked me right in the eye.

He said again, "No emotional attachments," as if to warn.

Then he kept going, trying to make sense of it. "She has friends and guests who come to the club just to see her."

I stayed calm and answered in a calm way. "I know that." She never tried to hide it. It didn't bother me.

After a while, I said, "She asked me not to come back." She was the one who called it quits. I don't think it's appropriate to judge her choices or make assumptions about her life there.

I let out a sigh.

I said softly, "That's not what shocks me." "It's how she got me. What I'm thinking. How I feel. Things I've never told anyone before. She knew all of them in some way."

I stopped talking and stared at the far horizon, lost in thought, before speaking again.

"I don't have any feelings for her and never will. But I appreciate that she was honest with me from the start. It seemed like she really cared about me."

I leaned back on the bench and took a deep breath. "That's all there is to it. Nothing more, nothing less."

My friend seemed worried. He leaned forward and said, "That's what she wanted. To make an impression on you. To make you think she's kind, honest, and respectful. And here you are, praising her right now."

He sighed, which indicated that he was upset. "Listen, don't trust too much too soon. I know you have a kind heart and it's hard for you to see things like this clearly. You don't know how this world works or the tricks women like her use, but I do. I've seen it all before. Just promise me you won't go back there or talk to her again."

I laughed a little to make things better. "I swear there's nothing between her and me. This is the second time I've told you this."

I said, "And anyway, I don't even have her number anymore," still smiling.

He frowned, but he kept going. "But she has yours, and that worries me."

I leaned back and told him not to worry. "Don't worry about me; I'm not that weak. I had a wonderful time talking to her, but that's all it was. She doesn't interest me in any other way."

He shook his head. "The problem is that she likes you for some reason."

I sighed in defense. "That's not true at all. She has been honest with me from the start. After our first meeting, she told me not to come back. When I did, she warned me again. What happened the last time I saw her? It's just to say goodbye. Nothing else happened. You don't need to worry."

My friend stopped talking when he realized I was upset. He chose not to keep talking.

I did not initially regard my friend's concerns with the appropriate seriousness, but his words lingered in my mind. I couldn't stop thinking about her. I started to feel strange.

I experienced a profound sense of restlessness. A need that can't be explained. Since I met Nadia, that feeling has only gotten stronger. She confused me because she could sense me in a way that no one else could. Now my friend's warnings made things even more confusing.

I didn't know who to trust. My friend thought Nadia was trying to control me, but she had always been honest with me. She only asked that I stay away from her. But I didn't believe anything because he wasn't sure.

What was most strange was how I felt so differently. I had always felt somewhat empty before. Like I was missing something in my life. But now that feeling had a name. Nadia. She was no longer just a passing thought. She had taken over my mind completely. And with that, a storm started to brew inside me.

At that point, I tried to ignore her. I pushed away every thought, memory, and thing that brought her back. However, the pain of not seeing her outweighed the pain of missing her. I felt like I was fighting with my mind. I had to give up something I didn't want to lose.

I learned a harsh truth. Avoidance is often more painful than pain itself. Suffering can be painful and emotional, but avoiding it is a constant battle to deny what can't be ignored.

This fight taught me something important. I could endure the pain when I wanted something else. The pain was merely a dull ache in the back of my head. But it hurt more that I couldn't have something that was right in front of me but out of reach. It felt like chasing a shadow. It was always in close proximity, yet it remained elusive.

I learned that ignorance can be beneficial. In a way, the unknown is safe. But knowing something is there and not being able to get it hurts a lot more. Not knowing isn't always a negative thing. It sometimes gently keeps our peace.

I wanted to see Nadia again and again. I even thought about putting on a disguise so she wouldn't know who I was. But I didn't do it in the end. I remembered what I had promised her. That meeting was really the last one we had. That I wouldn't be back.

I was slowly getting back to my normal life, but I couldn't stop thinking about her. She stayed in the background. A constant presence I couldn't get rid of. Even though I tried to focus on work, friends, or everyday things, she was still there. Like an unshakable shadow, it persistently lingered in the recesses of my mind.

I woke up late on Saturday. 3:00 PM. Sunlight coming through the curtains made the room feel warm. I checked my phone after I took a shower and got ready. That's when I noticed it. Nadia had sent texts. Without warning. I was shocked and stared at the screen. After all, she was the one who told me to stay away. She made me promise, too. Not one text, call, or trip to the club. I hadn't tried to get in touch with her. So why was she getting in touch now?

I felt many different things. I felt a mixture of happiness, worry, and uncertainty. I felt uneasy because my friend's warning kept playing in my head. Was this part of her plan? Was she trying to get me back, as he said? I stopped for a moment and then said, "Hi, I'm fine. How are you?"

She answered almost right away. "What are you doing?" I asked her what she was doing, and I told her that I had just woken up. She smiled and made fun of me for sleeping soundly when she couldn't. It felt different as we kept talking. The way she talked didn't sound like the Nadia I knew.

Then she sent a second message. "Should I get in touch with you?" I read her words very slowly. Things had changed. She had made up her mind to do things differently from now on. She wanted to know if I was upset with her for being mean during our last meeting. I told her not to worry about anything.

She said she was exhausted but had to get up at 7 AM. She said that talking to me made her feel better. It was like a weight had been taken off her mind. I softly told her to go to sleep. This made her feel better. I sent a thumbs-up emoji because I didn't know what else to say.

She was making me think about things I had been trying so hard to forget. It wasn't that I was afraid she would hurt me. The way I looked at her scared me. I thought those feelings were gone, but they kept coming back. My friend might have been right after all. She wasn't just trying to trick me. I wanted to keep the picture of her. The smart, kind, honest, and loving person I thought she was. That picture had become a calm place for my mind to rest in the middle of all the noise.

But now that her messages seem so different, I started to wonder if I had been right about her all along. Even though I had many thoughts going through my head, one question stayed. Why couldn't I stop thinking about her? How could I understand this other side of her that was different from the person I thought she was? What was our relationship, really, most importantly?

I didn't believe her when she said and did things that were just puzzles. It made me uneasy to think about it. Was she telling the truth, or was there something else going on? She seemed real, but the doubts my friend had put in my head wouldn't go away. How did she know so much about me? Things I had never told anyone before? I couldn't figure it out no matter how hard I tried. It seemed like she could see into my soul and point out things about me that I hadn't even thought about.

While I was having dinner with my friend, my phone buzzed with many messages from her. My heart skipped a beat. I tried to stay calm, but when I saw her name, I felt shocked and confused at the same time.

I couldn't pay attention while we ate. My friend kept talking, but I could hardly hear him. I couldn't stop thinking about her messages. Instead of enjoying the meal, I kept thinking about how to respond.

My friend looked calm and happy, but I was getting more and more anxious by the minute. Finally, I said, "I'm sorry, but I think we should end dinner now." I knew he wasn't going to leave anytime soon.

He was surprised when he looked at me. "Are you all right?"

"I don't feel good," I said.

He made a face. "What happened?"

"Nothing." I quickly stood up and said, "I just need some rest." He got up too, and not long after, I ran back to my room.

I fell onto the couch and unlocked my phone. There was another message from her.

"????"

It was easy, but it felt like it had to be done right away. My heart raced as I typed back.

"Hello."

"Good evening."

"I'm okay. How are you doing?"

She answered almost right away, as if she had been waiting.

"Did you have a lot to do?"

"Yes, a little."

"Did you already eat dinner?"

"Yes, I just finished."

She wrote, "Hmm, good." They were casual words, but something about them felt off.

Another message came after that.

"I want to talk to you sometimes, especially when I'm alone."

It took longer than usual. More weighty.

I knew this wasn't just a simple question. It felt like a door was opening. Calm, careful, but clear. She didn't ask directly, but I could tell she was waiting for a certain answer.

I stopped for a moment before answering. I would rather not say something wrong. Not only did I not want to agree to something she hadn't said, but I also didn't want to push her away.

For a moment, I typed, "I don't think I ever said that."

"Like what?" She asked.

"Like, stay away."

She said, "Hmmm," and left it open.

A new message came after I didn't answer.

"Well, you kept your word and stayed away."

I didn't say anything.

Then she asked, "Will you come if I ask?"

I said, "But I told you I wouldn't come back."

She answered right away.

"Yes, but now I'm asking you to. I'll wait for you tomorrow. Same place, same time."

I stared at the screen, and a heavy feeling settled in my chest. I couldn't just do things without thinking. But the pull was strong.

There was another message.

"Okay, I'm going on stage now." My phone will be turned off.

I sent a thumbs-up emoji, but I didn't feel good about it. I wanted to have a conversation with her. To say more. And more than anything, I didn't want her to go on stage.

The rest of the day went by with my mind racing. Should I leave or stay? The fight in my head made me tired. Logic pushed me in one direction. I felt pulled the other way. And deep down, I already knew what I wanted.

My friend's warnings kept coming back. The danger. The chance that she was playing games. Then there was her voice. She is being honest. The way she reached out was genuine. Everything seemed real. I told myself that it would be better to stay away. I wanted to keep my word to both her and myself. But as time went on, the pull got stronger.

I couldn't get rid of the feeling that this meeting was important. I felt that this meeting might finally provide me with the answers I needed.

I realized I was already there ten minutes before we were supposed to meet. In the same chair. At the same table. Like time had stopped. The café was quiet, with soft voices and the sound of glasses clinking. I was worried and excited as I waited for her to get there.

She got there sooner than she thought she would. She didn't even bother to ask if I was there. She walked in with confidence, as if nothing had changed between us. As she walked up to me, I stood up without thinking, as if I had done it a thousand times before.

She looked different today. More content. Less heavy. The whole time, she had a smile on her face. She was a little shy, which only made her more beautiful. Her hair was simple, with a loose strand falling over her cheek over and over again. She put it behind her ear, but it always fell back into place, as if it belonged there.

The small mole next to her soft pink lips stood out even more against her delicate features. My eyes were drawn to her without even trying. That little mark, which was faint but clear, felt special. It had a quiet meaning. It was something that made her unique and distinct.

She was aware that I was watching. She sat down slowly and calmly. It felt like she was letting me see every little thing on purpose. Each of her movements was slow and steady, and they all had a quiet confidence that made it difficult to look away.

She moved her chair a little bit. Her fingers touched the edge of the table. For a brief moment, our eyes met. We didn't say anything, but something passed between us. Then she turned away, her lips still curled in a soft smile.

At last, she spoke up.

"Do you know why I wanted to see you today?"

I didn't say anything and let her go on. I was nervous, but I didn't want to stop her.

"It started with our texts," she said quietly, her hands on the table. "But talking to each other didn't make everything clear for me."

"Like what?" I asked.

She stared at me. Her eyes were steady, but something was off. Maybe, not sure. Maybe feeling bad. As she spoke, her voice got a little lower.

"All I could say when you said you never told me to stay away was, 'Hmm.' Do you know how much one word can mean?"

"Yes," I said after a moment. "Sometimes it means you don't have anything to say and Sometimes it means you have too much to say but don't know how to say it."

"Exactly," she said. It looked like she was lost in thought because her eyes drifted away. Slowly, her fingers moved along the edge of the table.

"But what did your 'Hmm' mean?" I asked, leaning in. "I want to know."

She turned back to me and looked into my eyes. She thought I would get it without her having to say anything. I saw a crack in her confidence for the first time.

She said softly, "For me, it meant that sometimes you have to stay away from the things you want the most. Thinking distance is safer."

Her voice got softer, like it was about to break. It wasn't easy to find the words.

She stopped and looked past me for a moment. The silence between us grew heavy with all the things she wasn't saying.

Then she spoke again, but this time her voice was lower.

"Do you know what happens when you don't let out enough words?" She asked. Her voice shook. "They become snakes. They bite you from the inside. And every bite hurts."

The last word made her voice break. I could hear how much it hurt. This wasn't just a picture. She had been living with it for a while.

Today, she felt different. She had been smiling when she walked in, but now that smile felt weak. I could tell she was changing as we talked. She didn't have the confidence she usually did. She felt like something inside her had broken.

It seemed like she was trying to show me something that was very deep down. Something she would never show anyone. There were layers to what she said, and I wasn't sure I got them all.

Then she spoke again, this time in a softer voice.

"I might have sounded rude when I told you to stay away. I don't know what you thought about it."

I answered right away. "I never thought you were rude." I thought it was honest."

She turned away. She couldn't stop moving her fingers on the table. It looked like she was thinking about everything that had just happened.

"Yes," she said, "but it hurts when one person wants to talk and share, and the other person pulls back."

She stopped again.

I listened but didn't say anything. It felt like every word was true. She was letting me see a part of her that she had always kept secret.

We looked at each other again.

"Now you know why I told you to stay away, and why did not I want you to come here?" I only said, "Hmm."

She suddenly straightened up, forcing herself to take back control. Her hands were flat on the table. She took a deep breath before she spoke again.

"I won't stop you," she said. "You can come by anytime."

I didn't answer right away. The quiet settled between us. She looked away after our eyes met for a moment. Her fingers moved to her wrist, and the bangles on her wrist made a soft sound that filled the space between us.

I talked in a low voice. "The tears we hold back, the ones we don't let fall, are worse than words we don't say. They hurt a lot more."

She stopped moving. She quickly looked back at me. It looked like she wanted to say something for a second, but nothing came out. Instead, she held on tightly to the edge of the table.

I didn't wait for her to answer. I lit a cigarette, took a slow drag, and let the smoke drift between us, covering everything we hadn't said.

"I have to tell you something," she said.

Her voice was shaky, but it was strong enough to keep my full attention. "To be honest, I was more worried about myself than about you. I get what you're saying, but I also know who I am. It was hard for me to stay away from you. And I stayed away from you on purpose. You can understand it any way you want."

Her words stayed between us, heavy and true. I didn't say anything. I just looked at her and searched her eyes for something I couldn't put into words. I wanted to say a lot, but I couldn't because she told me what she did.

She spoke again, but this time it was quieter.

"Time is running out."

She got up to go. She paused, as if she had no choice but to leave, but it looks as she didn't want to. For a moment, she stayed there with her hand on the back of the chair. Our eyes met for a moment. I felt like I was being pulled toward her, but I also felt like something was pulling her away.

That day was different. I knew she wouldn't leave easily.

My mind was racing as I sat there. Did my being there have the same effect on her as being there had on me? She wants to meet. The quiet she had. Her admission. Everything started to make sense. Maybe she was going through the same thing I was, but from a different angle.

Around her, time always seemed strange. When she was around, time flew by. The world slowed down, which gave us room to live. But I felt like something was still missing when she left. Words that never got out.

But every time she sat down in front of me, I shut up. Her presence completely engulfed me. Being with her made me feel calm in a way I had never felt before. I stopped worrying. I could only see her. Her eyes. Her smile. Her kindness.

The little mole on her face was like a secret. Something that only she had. A small thing that made her seem more real and human. At those times, it seemed like everything was about her. Time. Pretty. Life itself. I felt a kind of happiness I hadn't felt in a long time.

It felt like a door opening when she said I could see her anytime. One I didn't know was closed. I felt better. It felt like a weight had been taken off of me without me knowing it. The doubt in my mind started to go away for the first time in weeks.

I thought she felt something too, even though neither of us said it out loud. It felt like the beginning of a new chapter. One that is full of possibilities.

I walked home that night with my mind on other things. I did not wish for her to depart, just as I did not wish for the song to conclude. When I reflected on her, I experienced a lingering warmth within me long after we parted ways.

When I woke up the next morning, I saw a simple message.

"Good morning."

They said two words, but they meant more than that. They made my mornings meaningful and my evenings peaceful.

Those messages connected us in some way. Something steady in the middle of not knowing. I experienced improvement each time I received one, yet I also felt apprehensive about what might occur subsequently.

As time went on, I realized how deeply she listened. She demonstrated a profound level of care. It was a relief to have her in my life. Even from afar, her presence brought peace and clarity.

Following that day, she never requested my return, but I still wished to see her. The need grew stronger as the days went by. I finally sent her a message.

"Can we get together?"

She just said, "Yes, why not?"

I thought about it for a second, then said, "Not at the café."

She took longer to answer this time. Then there was one word.

"Where?"

I said, "Somewhere outside." We could go to the beach, the desert, or just walk down the street.

After a short break, she said, "You know I can't." I can't leave. "Please let me."

I couldn't hide it when I wrote, "I want to see you today."

"Today?" She asked, surprised.

"Yes, please."

"Please give me some time," she said.

"Okay," I said, gripping my phone tightly.

She wrote, "Okay," thirty minutes later. We can walk down the street.

I said, "Thank you," and felt better.

She said, "I'll wait for you at the hotel." "Then we'll walk."

I sent a thumb-up, and my heart raced.

I got there early and waited in the café. I saw her walking toward me fifteen minutes before our time. She glanced at the ashtray and then at me.

"When did you arrive?" She asked in a casual way, but her eyes were sharp.

"Fifteen minutes ago," I said.

She looked at the ashtray again, as if she were counting the cigarettes. Then she shook her head a little. She looked a little disappointed.

She had on a kurta, jeans, and a small dupatta around her neck. Easy. Pretty. Totally herself. The outfit fit her perfectly.

I couldn't stop staring. Trying to remember everything. The way the light hit her hair. Her eyes held a multitude of unspoken thoughts.

"Let's go," she said.

I smiled and said, "Let's go."

When we went outside, the cool evening air brushed our faces. She walked next to me like it was something we did all the time.

The road was lined with trees, and their branches swayed gently in the wind.

I kept looking at her. The streetlights made her face look softer and gave her an almost otherworldly glow.

There were no cars on the road. The leaves that were dry crunched under our feet. It felt like we were in our own world because the light was warm and there was no sound.

I said softly, "I don't want this to happen." "I never asked for it, but it's happening anyway." I don't know why.

I stopped moving. I gazed at her, seeking clarity. I was searching for answers.

"You know me so well," I said again. "Do you understand why I feel this way?"

For a moment, she didn't say anything. Then she said, "Go ahead." You can smoke if you like.

I lit up a cigarette. She didn't say anything else right away.

She said calmly, "If someone else told me this, I'd say they're in love."

What she said made something in my chest tighten.

"But you're not like that," she said.

"You live in a world you made," she said. "Where people are honest and loyal." But that world isn't real.

She gave me a careful look.

"I wish I hadn't told you the truth about my life." I thought you would hate me. But you called it being honest.

She let out a sigh.

"That's why I told you not to come near." I knew the truth would hurt you.

I spoke softly.

"Being with you feels like answers." Like everything is clear.

She paid attention.

She said, "I knew you didn't belong there when I first saw you." People don't think we're real. "They only see what they can get."

She looked down.

"It felt different with you. It calms me to talk to you.

We walked for almost an hour. Be quiet. Next to each other.

We stopped for tea and sat there without talking. The warmth was enough.

I said "thank you" at the door of the hotel.

She smiled. "Thanks too."

On that day, I chose not to bother her. Sometimes caring means being far away.

We stayed away from the club. We sent each other casual messages.

Then, one night, she called me on video.

"Do you miss me?" She asked in a playful way.

"Yes," I said.

"Why haven't you come?"

"Should I?"

She made a joke. "No... not really."

"I'll be there soon," I said.

"I'll be waiting," she said in a soft voice.

When I told my friend the next day that I was going back, he said very seriously,

"I told you so."

I didn't say anything. I couldn't defend myself. No reason.

And he was aware of it.

He kept trying to talk me out of going to the club as we drove there. But I sat still and let his words wash over me.

I couldn't stop thinking about how she would react when she saw me. I was nervous but also hopeful. The words I had read days before kept coming back to me. "Let your heart slowly move toward what it really wants; it will never lead you astray."

She smiled widely when I got to the club. Just looking at her made my heart stop racing. It felt like time stopped when I played her songs that night. Nothing else mattered at that moment except her smile and the music that filled the room. All of my problems went away.

After that, I started going to the club almost every day. Usually, I went by myself, but occasionally my friend came with me. I'd leave early so no one would see me. Listen to music. Keep an eye on Nadia from a distance. I incorporated it into my daily routine, and it temporarily improved my mood.

But I quickly realized that I needed Nadia to be happy. She was the center of my life. It felt as if she could fill the hole in my heart.

My friend came into my house one day, clearly angry. He hardly said hello before asking, "What are you doing?"

His voice was loud and full of blame. I didn't care about how he sounded, so I turned around. "Nothing," I said calmly, but with caution.

"Nothing?" He turned back, getting angrier. "You're at the club every day now. What's going on? Why are you so obsessed all of a sudden?"

I didn't say anything. How could I put it? He wouldn't get it. He couldn't see or feel what I did.

He let out a sigh. His voice got a little softer, but he was still furious. "I'm not worried about how much money you're spending. I'm worried about you. This is going to ruin you."

"How?" I asked in a calm voice. Almost not there.

He took a deep breath and ran his fingers through his hair. "She's going to break you. That's how these things work. She's trained for this. This is her job. She's not there for love. She's there for money. Do you understand?"

I stared at him, and my face didn't change. "No. She's not like anyone else. No one else is like her."

He gave me a hard look. His eyes were looking for any sign that I was weak in my resolve. He groaned again when he couldn't find any. This time, there was a hint of helplessness.

"Okay, then try it. Keep going to the club, but don't ask for any songs for a few days. Don't spend any money on her. Just watch and see what happens."

"What will happen?" I asked.

He said, "She won't even notice you." His voice had a bitter edge to it. "Her smiles and friendliness are only for people who give her money. The truth is, she doesn't think about you at all."

He saw things in a way that I couldn't, like many other people. He didn't see anything in her that was like what I went through.

"What's your real concern? Why does this bother you so much?" I asked him to think.

"She'll ruin you," he said with no emotion. "This fantasy will make you lose yourself, and for what? For someone who doesn't care at all? You'll be good for nothing."

I pushed, "How?" My voice was still calm.

His tone got harsher. "These women aren't loyal. How many times do I have to tell you? They're not like us. They see and feel things in a different way."

I asked again, "So the real problem is that they're not loyal?"

"Yes," he said without thinking.

I grabbed a glass of water from the table. I held it lightly in my hand while I talked. The glass's coolness brought me back to earth. Letting me think things over.

"What if I told you I'm not emotionally attached? What if I'm just passing time with her? What if I only want something physical and nothing more? Would that be okay?"

He moved around in his chair. His face relaxed a little. What I said had alleviated some of his worries.

"Yeah, then it's fine. No problem," he said. He sounds more relaxed now.

I drank some water. I couldn't help but smile slightly. I couldn't help but see the irony. How easily he let me use her. As if it were the most normal thing in the world.

When he saw me smile, he frowned. "What's so funny?"

"Nothing," I said. My voice was calm, but there was a hint of humor in it.

He leaned forward, spoke in a low, serious voice, and seemed determined to make his point. "You smile because you don't know her tricks. You think you and she are special, but you're not."

But this wasn't just what he thought. Most people agreed with it.

It's okay for a man to use a woman. Society agrees. Even society agrees. But what if he loves her? If he has the guts to say he loves her? That's not right. That doesn't seem right.

People don't question a man when he says he's slept with a woman. No one thinks badly of him. They might even call him a player and a champion and praise him. But what if he tells her he loves her? People think it's weird. People say he's naive. Make fun of him. Make fun of him. Tell him he's wrong.

I looked at my friend. My voice was calm, but it was also defiant.

"I don't know what a woman means to you or what you want from them. But for me, it's different. I'm not attracted to her body; I respect her mind, her words, her presence, and how she feels about me. I haven't even thought about whether she's loyal or not, but the peace I find with her is enough for me."

I took a big breath. I stared straight ahead, as if I were testing his knowledge.

"What surprises me most is this way of thinking. If I told you I used Nadia and slept with her, you wouldn't mind. You might even nod or laugh. But if I say that I like her because she makes me feel good, is that considered wrong? Why? Because you're afraid she'll hurt me? Or because you're afraid I might be happy?"

After that, my friend didn't say anything. He just sat there and looked at me. You couldn't read his face. The room got quiet. My words are heavy in the air.

I thought I had won the argument with my friend because he stopped talking, but I still felt like what I was saying wasn't entirely true. I really appreciated Nadia's loyalty, even though I would rather not say it out loud. I knew I was being too possessive of her, but I kept denying it. I'm putting up more of a fight to convince myself than anyone else.

I wanted to name my feelings a lot. I wanted to tell her that she was the most important person in my life. The word "love" occupied my mind often, even if I never spoke it aloud. Maybe I wanted her to say it first, deep down. I was afraid that saying it would break the weak bond we had.

Thereafter, I got busy and missed a few days at the club. At first, everything seemed fine. We continued our conversations through talking and texting, but I began to observe that her behaviour was changing.

It began small. Not very noticeable. There is a delay in the response. There was a shorter conversation. But it became clear over time. Even though I could tell things were getting worse, I couldn't bring myself to ask her about it. I might not have wanted to hear the answer. I might have been scared of what it could mean.

She didn't talk to me as much. She used to always have something to say. A tale. A view. A query. Our talks would end quickly, and she wouldn't pick them up again. She wouldn't call back if the call dropped. She'd text later to say she had fallen asleep.

It hurt more and more, not because anything was happening to me, but because the picture of her in my mind was fading. She was beautiful, smart, kind, caring, and honest with me. That picture was slowly falling apart now.

I made the decision to go to the club one day. She smiled when she first saw me, but it seemed like she was trying too hard. I sat still and didn't ask for a song. I noticed that she was looking at me less over time. Not smiling as much.

I couldn't stop thinking about the question. What made her act this way?

I wasn't sure if I should stay or leave, but I finally did. I wasn't mad at her. She never said she loved me. But I kept thinking. What was wrong with Nadia?

I went home with a heavy heart. I started to think that the world was darker than I had ever thought. That in the end, money was all that mattered, and feelings didn't matter at all.

I lay in bed at home trying to sleep. I didn't know what I was feeling. Or maybe I just wasn't ready to deal with it.

I woke up just before dark, and for some reason, I wasn't thinking about her. When I got up to go out to dinner, my phone rang. She called me on video.

I wasn't sure if I should answer, so I waited. My finger was just above the screen. I couldn't stop thinking about how far apart we were. Then I chose to pick up.

She wanted to know how I was. It felt as if nothing had happened the night before. She smiled and said hello to me. Her voice was warm and familiar, but the way she spoke seemed off. It seemed like she was trying too hard to keep things light.

"Once you told me I was completely unique," I said, not sure why.

She nodded, and her gaze softened. "You really are."

I kept going. My voice was calm, but I couldn't help but feel heavy. "You also told me that the world you live in is very dark."

"Yes," she said softly.

"I used to not be afraid of this darkness, but now I think I am," I said, taking a deep breath. As I got ready to say what had been bothering me, my chest tightened.

She looked surprised. Her eyes got a little bigger. But she didn't say anything.

I stopped for a moment and then spoke again. Now my voice is softer. "I know this might upset you, but I'm not the first or last person in your life. Nothing could really change you. Nothing that would bring about the peace I feel with you."

She took a deep breath and said, "I don't know why you're saying this, but what if I told you you're the first and last in my life?"

I barely saw it, but I smiled a little. "I'd say you're lying."

She stopped. Her eyes were steady, but they were also open. Then she said softly, "What you've given me, no one else has. Maybe no one else could. Respect. In this world, we're treated like trash, but it's what we want most. Everyone just wants to take us to their rooms. Nothing more. But when you look at me, your eyes don't show lust. They show respect. And that makes me feel seen and valued in a way I've never felt before."

This was the first time someone had ever said something like that to me. Her words were like a warm hug that stayed with me. Even through the screen. Coming out of my phone's speakers.

I was no longer frustrated. It was replaced by a strange, painful feeling of helplessness. It was the understanding of something I'd never fully understood before. How much a person wants to be noticed. To hear that they're special. Not the same. It wasn't just about saying sweet things or making empty promises. It was about feeling loved in a way that no one else could.

"Nadi," I said. My voice is quiet. Almost shy. "You know me well..."

Her face was frozen on the screen. Her eyes got bigger. It was as if the word struck her like lightning. "What did you just call me?" she said in a voice that was almost a whisper. Carrying shock or nostalgia. Possibly both.

I hesitated because I wasn't sure. "Nadi, I'm sorry if you don't like it."

She shook her head quickly. Her lips moved as if she wanted to say something, but at first, no words came out. Then she said in a soft voice, "No, no. It's just Nadi. That's what my mom calls me."

I could see the emotions in her eyes even though the screen was pixelated. Her voice shook. For a moment, she looked away. It was as if she were trying to calm herself down. But the way she looked showed that she was weak.

She turned back to the camera before she could cry. You could barely hear her voice. "What were you talking about?"

I took a big breath. I was having trouble putting my feelings into words, and my chest was getting tighter. "You know me very well. You also know that I tend to overthink things and am very possessive. You probably also know how hard it is to be with someone like that. Maybe that's why I've always felt so alone."

She stared at me. Her face showed both worry and confusion. "Why are you saying all this?"

I tripped. She didn't understand that what I said, how I felt, and how I reacted to her behaviour were all the same as what she did. She didn't know it very well either.

I was thinking quickly, trying to find a way to connect with you. After a short pause, I asked, "Do you remember how long we used to talk? What happened? Why don't you talk to me like you used to?"

She looked at me playfully, but there was still a hint of sadness in her eyes. "You think I'm ignoring you?"

I didn't say anything because I didn't know what to say. The truth was that I didn't know how to show how much pain I was in. How her distance had made me feel lost.

She let out a sigh. Her shoulders went down a little. It felt like the weight of her whole world was on her. "How can I explain the problems we have every day? Our families only talk to us when they need something. We're not stone; we're human. There's trouble at home. There are always demands and pressure."

She sounded worn out. And for the first time, I saw how heavy her burdens were. These were burdens that she had never mentioned to me before.

She stopped for a moment. Before she spoke, her eyes wandered away. "Talking to you helps me calm down when everything is too much. It reminds me that at least one person talks to me for no other reason."

"But you too," she said, but then she stopped in the middle of the sentence. Her voice broke, and for the first time, I saw tears in her eyes.

I sat up straighter, and my heart raced. "Are you crying, Nadi?" She shook her head and wiped away her tears quickly. "No."

I got closer to the screen. Speaking softly but with strength. "Nadi, you're smart and strong. Are you really falling apart?"

She took a big breath. She stood up straight, but her eyes were still shining. "No, I'm not crying."

But I could see what was really going on. And for the first time, I comprehended how anguish it is to witness someone you cherish in tears. I experienced a sharp sensation in my chest. I experienced a sharp pain that made it hard for me to breathe.

I swallowed hard. My voice was barely above a whisper. "I'm sorry, Nadi. I never meant for this to happen."

She gave me a look. Her voice got softer all of a sudden. Almost breakable. "I can't explain it, but talking to you makes me feel better in a way that nothing else does."

I stopped talking. I feel like guilt is a stone on my chest. Someone was crying for the first time because of me. That thought hurt more than anything else I'd ever felt. I couldn't get rid of the pain. This served as a reminder of how much my words and actions could hurt her.

She said softly but firmly, "No one has ever held the place you hold in my heart before, and maybe no one ever will." It was like she was trying to comfort me even though she was feeling bad herself.

I didn't say anything because I didn't know what to say.

She spoke again after that. Her voice was careful. It was as if her words echoed your own thoughts. "In my world, trust is hard to come by. No one believes in anyone. Maybe they shouldn't. But we're still human. Our hearts still beat. We need love and respect, not just money. We have feelings too, and occasionally we want to give someone a piece of our heart."

For a moment, we were both quiet. The silence between us felt heavier than words. It was full of unexpressed thoughts and unspoken feelings.

This silence, which connected us even through the screen, said a lot.

At last, I spoke up. "Nadi." "Hmm?" she said softly. Through the phone, her eyes meet mine.

"You just said that no one else has or ever will hold the place in your heart that I do." "That's true," she said right away.

"I said, "Promise me something." My voice is shaky, but it's honest. "Of course, tell me," She said. Her voice was soft but focused.

"Do what you want when I'm not there. But don't pay more attention to anyone else than you do to me when I'm there. Don't shake hands with anyone. I dont know, but it really hurts me"

"First of all, I always stay on stage, whether you're there or not," she said with a small laugh. It was warm and familiar. "Second, why would I shake hands with someone else if I've never done it with you? But I promise I won't if it matters to you."

I looked at her face on the screen. The way her smile curved. The way her eyes softened when she spoke. The faint glimmer of tears remained in her eyes. I wanted to freeze this moment and keep it close forever.

I wanted to say so much more, but all I could say was "Thank you."

She nodded and smiled quietly, as if she knew what was going on. "It's time for me to go."

The call abruptly ended, erasing the closeness I had experienced moments earlier. The screen darkened, leaving me alone with my thoughts.

She was so strangely beautiful that even though I knew everything that was true and made every point I could, I started to doubt my own judgment. Reason seemed powerless in her presence. Some forces just rule; they don't make their case. I accepted the pain, I wanted to absorb every beauty, she holds.

6

For the first time, I asked Nadi for something, and she said yes. I never thought I would feel safe because of her promise. That promise broke down the wall of worry and doubt I had built around myself, letting in a little bit of light that I didn't know I needed. It wasn't really about what she did. It was a matter of trust. It was about the bond that is silently growing between us.

After that, I stopped contemplating whether or not to go to the club. I no longer felt the fear and doubt that had previously held me back. They were replaced by a feeling of freedom that I hadn't had in years. I permitted myself to fully enjoy being with her without concern for my words or actions. Don't think too much about it. My fears vanished, and for the first time, I truly experienced the present moment.

Was I falling in love? Every night before I went to sleep, I thought about Nadi. Every morning when I woke up, she was the first thing on my mind. She was always there. No matter where I went or what I did, they were always in my heart and mind. I let myself feel everything for the first time without holding back. It was scary, but it was also exciting.

One thing I started noticing very soon. Nadi started talking to me more when I started going to the club more often. It felt like her words were softer. More personal. It was as if she was gradually opening a door to a part of her life that she seldom revealed to others. We even started calling each other late at night after the club closed, sometimes until one of us fell asleep. Her voice made me feel better. Her voice served as a constant source of light in my chaotic life.

My daily routine included our calls over time. It wasn't just about the club anymore. Nadi opened up to me in ways that made me feel special. Every day, I looked forward to talking to her. Her voice either put me to sleep or kept me company until the early hours of the morning.

It seemed like her thoughts stayed with me even when she was on stage. What we shared extended beyond the club. It was there, but not there. True, but fragile. And I wanted to do everything I could to keep it safe.

I have observed that most of the guest means special rich guest used to come late at night. I began to get there early and leave early to keep things safe. I made sure not to engage in any unnecessary drama. I made sure not to allow things to spiral out of control. I wanted to keep us both safe and focus on what was important: our time together. Every time we talked, I liked her more and more.

I didn't want anything in particular from her. I only wanted her. Every second with her felt important. Every minute we were apart seemed like an eternity. I wanted her to be there. Her focus. I wanted her to give whatever she was willing to give.

I lost control one day. I had to hear Nadi's voice. I knew she would be sleeping in the middle of the day, but I still called. Every ring made my heart race, and each one was louder than the last. I heard her sleepy voice just as I was about to hang up.

"Hey?"

My heart stopped for a second. I said, "Hi, Nadi," trying to hide how happy I was.

"Hello," she said in a soft, foggy voice, as if she were still half asleep.

I felt better right away. "I'm so glad you picked up," I said, and just hearing her voice made the tension in my chest go away.

She stopped for a moment. The phone picked up the soft sound of the blankets as she moved around in bed. "Is everything all right?"

"Yes. I just wanted to hear your voice. "I missed you."

She made a soft sound that was somewhere between a laugh and a sigh. It was relaxing to be quiet with each other. It was like we didn't need words to understand each other.

I took a deep breath and finally said what I had been holding back for so long, even though my heart was still racing.

"Nadi, I have to tell you something. I Love you. I don't know if this is the right time, but I can't keep it to myself any longer."

Be quiet. Heavy and long. My heart raced. Did I go too fast? Did I say too much?

After a while, I asked in a soft voice, "Do you have nothing to say?"

She spoke softly, as if she were carefully picking each word.

"How I feel about you is different. I don't know if I love you. I've never felt like this before. "I love you if this is love."

Her words wrapped around me like a hug. It wasn't just what she said. It was her truthfulness. She was genuine and her voice was quiet.

I smiled and spoke more softly. "Thanks, Nadi."

"Okay," she said, sounding a little funny. "But is this the only way you think we should show love?" "I could hear the smile in her voice."

I really felt like I had found what I had been looking for. I experienced a sense of belonging that was beyond words. It wasn't about giving or getting. Being with Nadi was enough. That's what I thought.

I took her love with me everywhere I went. It made my days warmer and gave me a sense of peace. I knew I wasn't the only one. Her voice, her words, and her presence were always a source of peace for me.

We were on the phone one day, and when I tried to call her back later, her phone was off. Right away, worry set in. I couldn't sit still all day, and my mind kept going over the worst things that could happen.

That night, she finally texted me. "Good evening." I felt a wave of relief. But when we talked, she hardly brought up the missed call, as if nothing had happened. I didn't like how casual she sounded.

When I asked her what had happened to her phone, she didn't seem to care. "It's fine." But I couldn't let it go. She finally admitted that her phone had fallen and stopped working after a moment of hesitation. She was texting me from a coworker's phone.

I didn't think about it much before I decided to resolve the problem. I went to the market that night and got her a new phone. I thought about surprising her at the bar. The way she smiled. What she did. There was thankfulness in her eyes.

But when I got there with the gift, she didn't react the way I thought she would. She seemed shocked but not happy. Something else came over her face. Maybe pain. Or rage. I couldn't say.

I gave her the phone without saying much. She looked at it for a second, then left the stage and went into the back room. I stood there, confused, for longer than I should have. Something was different when she got back.

She smiled every now and then, but she seemed far away. She wouldn't look me in the eye. She wouldn't let me in, no matter how hard I tried. It seemed like she had put up a wall between us.

I didn't get it. I just wanted to show her how much I cared.

I told a friend what had happened later. He didn't say anything, but his demeanour got more serious with each word I said. He let out a long sigh when I was done, as if he had been holding it in the whole time.

"Let me tell you what this is," he said with confidence. "She probably thought it would be something pleasing. Something that is the best. She didn't want what you gave her; she wanted something else. Not a normal phone."

I didn't say anything. I didn't know what to say. His words hit me like a punch to the stomach, but I couldn't help but see that they made some strange sense.

"She's playing you," he said in a sharp voice. "Her old phone is probably fine." She made you think it was broken so she could get something from you.

What he said made sense, but it seemed mean. Was Nadi really using me, or was there something else going on?

I got stuck in a weird state of mind. Everything seemed murky. There were times when Nadi's words seemed honest and real, but there were also times when her actions made me question everything.

I didn't get what was going on.

Every time I tried to get close to her and trust her, she did something that made me lose that trust. And just when I was about to leave, she would act completely differently. Even the way she spoke would change.

I couldn't tell what she wanted or what she was really trying to do.

I felt like she had locked me up.

The prison walls were fake feelings, and the chains were empty promises. I couldn't get away from either one of them.

It hurt deeply every time my trust was broken and my feelings were hurt.

Someone seemed to be testing my limits.

One night I was sitting far away and watching her. Nadi kept glancing at the door. Every time I looked at her, her face changed. It seemed like she was waiting for someone.

Then she smiled. She got up and walked over to three new people who had just come in near the stage. She hugged one of them and shook hands with the other two.

For a second, I didn't know what I had just seen. It was difficult to breathe. The air around me felt thick. I kept my eyes on Nadi, hoping she would look at me. Hoping she would see that I was there.

But she didn't. Not even once.

She laughed and leaned in as they talked, completely focused on them. Every move made my worst fears come true. This was not the same. She talked to them differently than she did to me.

I kept looking, hoping that our eyes would meet. I had the question ready. What are you doing? What are you doing?

But that time never came.

She never looked at me. Not even by chance. She was completely focused on them, and her laughter filled the room.

Thereafter, the music started, and her show began.

Nadi walked onto the stage with a new kind of grace.

I had seen her dance a lot. I thought I knew how to do everything. But this was different. This wasn't the Nadi I knew.

The way she walked onto the stage,

the way her eyes met the crowd and softened with a smile,

the way the music made every movement flow.

The way she smiled. The light in her eyes was captivating.

Everything was new to me.

That day, I learned something.

Dancing is not the same as moving your body.

The difference felt like love, importance, or choice. Maybe something even more profound. That was all I knew at the time.

I couldn't figure out what had happened for a while. It felt like being hit out of the blue. You can't feel anything in your body, and you don't even know where it hurts.

This was the only thing I knew. I had been hurt badly.

I would find out later where the wound was and how deep it was.

It seemed like I should leave. I really did. But my legs wouldn't move. My heart wouldn't let go. I only needed one look from her. One look showed that I still mattered.

She didn't look at me once during all the songs. It felt like I wasn't there.

The visitors stood up when she was done with her performance. Nadi left the stage and went right to them. She shook hands and hugged one of them again.

The room felt heavier. Everything became fuzzy. I kept looking at her, trying to figure it out. She looked calm. Normal. As if I wasn't even there.

She finally went back to her seat. For a split second, our eyes met.

She then turned away.

I still couldn't feel anything. I didn't know yet that a wave of pain was coming.

I got up. I couldn't sit down any longer. I paid the bill and left the club without talking to her.

The air outside felt cleaner, but my head was a mess. There was a change between us. I didn't know what was going on or why.

The night was colder than it usually is. The streets were quiet, as if everyone in the world had stopped to watch me fall apart.

Then my phone rang.

It was Nadi.

I couldn't answer because my heart raced. I let it ring. She called again. And once more. Finally, a message arrived.

"Please, cafe."

I said, "Okay." I don't know why. It could have been the numbness.

I went to the cafe with a heavy chest and many questions in my head.

Nadi came a little while later.

She was not the same. She took her time and was more careful with her steps. She stopped for a moment before sitting down. She moved her chair closer to mine when she sat.

But the space between us seemed too big to cross.

I didn't stand up when she came today. I stayed in my seat. My hands were on the table. I kept looking at her.

At first, she didn't say anything. She kept her head down. She looked up every now and then, but she couldn't hold my gaze.

There was something in her eyes that I couldn't name. Maybe she couldn't say she was sorry.

She reached for my hand.

I pulled back.

She tried again, getting closer and waiting for me to answer.

I couldn't.

She looked at me one last time, looking for something. A response, a message.

Then she turned away and played with her bangles. The soft sound broke the silence and made the space between us seem even bigger.

We were in the same room, but we were in different worlds.

Finally, she spoke up and broke the silence.

"I'm sorry."

I didn't say anything.

She looked at me again, and her eyes were full of something I couldn't figure out.

"I'm sorry," she said again, this time with a softer tone.

The numbness went away. The pain came.

I clenched my hands under the table. My jaw got tight. I wanted to scream, but I couldn't.

And then I understood.

The wound wasn't in another place.

It went straight through my heart.

And it was very deep.

My mind was racing with a thousand questions. Why did you do this? Why did everything seem like a lie? And why did you ask me to come to the cafe again? But I couldn't get the words out. I knew that if I said anything, I would fall apart. Because of this, I stayed quiet. I was hoping she would say something. I was looking for anything that could help me understand the situation better.

The air between us became too much to handle. Nadi kept checking her phone. It seemed as if she was either looking for a way to leave or checking the time.

She finally spoke after what felt like an eternity.

It was difficult to hear her voice. "I have to leave."

I didn't say anything while she turned away. No goodbyes. The only thing I could hear was her footsteps fading.

I stayed there for a while, looking at the empty chair she had left behind. The quiet was heavier than it had ever been. I kept going over everything in my head, looking for answers that weren't there.

I lit a cigarette and took a drag. That was when I recognized that my body and mind were already overwhelmed with pain, rendering me unable to endure the smoke.

Smoking used to calm me down. It hurts today. I tried to take another drag, but I couldn't. I put the cigarette out in the ashtray.

I finally got up and left the cafe. I walked under the streetlights, but even though they were bright, everything inside me felt dark. I walked around without a plan. All I knew was that I had to keep going. It felt like grief was pulling me down with every step.

Then the pain got too bad.

I stopped. Sat down on the side of the road. I held my head with both hands, as if I were trying to keep myself together. I thought my head would explode. The stress kept getting worse. I held on tighter, hoping it would stop, but it only got worse.

And then I lost it.

I yelled. Very loud. Not cooked. Not in control. The sound bounced off the empty street and faded away into the night.

After that, I sat there, exhausted and out of breath. The pain had gotten as bad as it could get. I think I would have passed out if it had gotten any stronger.

Then it started to go away slowly.

As soon as I got home, I went to bed. I was completely exhausted.

I got up late the next day. I missed work. I couldn't make myself go. I couldn't get Nadi out of my head, and my friend's words kept coming back to me. I couldn't get away from them no matter how hard I tried.

I stayed away from everyone for days. I stayed in my room by myself, and my mind kept going over the same questions.

Was it really about the money? I would have given it to her if she needed it. So, why all the games? Were those times we had together fake?

What confused me the most was how hard she worked at it. Why put in so much effort for something that wasn't real? How could someone be so talented at acting?

The thoughts never stopped coming. They kept going around in my head.

A few days later, my friend came to see how I was doing. I tried to act like everything was fine. I spoke as if everything was fine. But he knew me too well. He could see how much it hurt.

He kept telling us to go out. A club. Anyplace. But I didn't want to be around people. I wanted peace and quiet.

He knew what had happened, but he wanted me to tell him. He looked at my face and asked carefully.

"Did you talk to Nadi?"

I didn't say anything.

This time, he asked again, more firmly. "Did you talk to Nadi?"

I looked at him but didn't say anything.

He got up, made coffee, and gave me a cup. When he gave it to me, he said, "Your eyes are saying everything. You don't have to explain. I told you this would ruin you. You wouldn't even know when it happened."

I took a deep breath and drank the coffee. I said, "It's over. I don't have anything against her."

I stopped for a moment and then went on. "I only have one thing I wish I could change. I wish that someone like Nadi hadn't been responsible for all of this. What really hurts isn't what happened. I let myself get close to her. "I shouldn't have."

I saw the steam coming out of my cup. "The picture I had of her. Pretty. Smart. Kind. Affectionate. It's no longer there. I wish I could have saved that picture. How I first saw her.

He stayed quiet and listened. Then he asked in a soft voice, "What happened?"

I shook my head. "Nothing." I should have paid attention to you. "Nadi told me how dark this world is." My voice got lower. "But I didn't believe her. She was more than I had hoped for. She felt at peace. She was more than just a body. She was intelligent. "Every word she said had meaning."

I looked down at my cup and tightened my grip on it. "I'm not sad because she lied to me or played games with me. It's sad that someone like Nadi was involved in lies at all.

For a while, we just sat there in silence.

Then I spoke again, calm but heavy. "Everyone has one person in their life who means everything to them. Nobody else matters after them. For me, that person was Nadi. No one is after her.

My friend was shocked. He slowly put his cup down. "You loved her that much."

I looked at him and started to cry. I tried to keep the tears from coming, but my hands shook, and the cup shook.

"She was my heart."

7

Nadi kept trying to get in touch with me. Her texts came in bursts. Sometimes sorry. Other times, they act as if nothing happened. She would send a text that said, "Good morning," and then "How are you? Can we talk?" She called when I didn't answer. I would just look at her name on my screen. I was about to press the answer button, but I couldn't do it. The sound of her ringtone, which used to make me happy, now twisted something deep inside my chest.

She didn't stop. She sent voice messages. Her voice was soft, like she was begging. "Please, just talk to me," she said. "I need to explain."

But what was there to explain? I had seen it all. How she acted toward them. Her laugh. The promise she didn't keep. Even though her words sounded honest, they couldn't change what I had seen with my own eyes.

But she kept going. One night, she sent a long message. She really let herself go. She said, "I know I hurt you, and I'm sorry, but you don't know the truth. You are very important to me. Please, just give me one chance to make it right." I read it over and over again. My heart was torn in two. Some of me wanted to trust her. To give her that chance. But the broken part of me wouldn't let me do it.

I kept doing what I always do. Going to work. Going for a hike. Going for long walks. Not answering her calls. I thought that keeping busy would help me forget about her. I stayed late at work and did things that didn't really matter. I pushed myself on hikes, climbing higher and going farther, hoping that being physically tired would make the pain go away. At night, I walked slowly through empty streets. The cool air brushed my face, and my thoughts kept me company.

But no matter what I did, Nadi stayed with me. I remembered her smile out of the blue. I could still hear her voice in my head.

She was everywhere. I tried so hard to get away from her, but I couldn't.

I told myself I didn't care anymore, but I still looked at my phone. I told myself I wouldn't answer, but the silence between us was heavy. When I didn't hear from her for a long time, a sharp pain reminded me how much I missed her. I wanted to forget about her, but I couldn't stand the thought of her forgetting about me.

Nadi was now a part of me. Not someone who just passed by. She was a part of my thoughts, feelings, and habits. She kept something alive in me. Every second we spent together changed me. It felt like something had been taken from me now that she was gone. Something that couldn't be replaced. Nothing else could fill the space that her absence left.

It felt impossible to move on, no matter how hard I tried. The more I tried to forget her, the more I remembered her.

Her face. The sound of her voice. How she made me feel. Everything came back with the same strength, making it hard for me to let go.

I felt like I was stuck. Wanting to move on but not being able to. I tried harder every day, and every day it hurt more. She stayed with me no matter how far I went.

I finally began to accept something I didn't want to deal with. A person like Nadi could never really be committed. Over and over, I heard her words, saw her actions, and thought about her patterns. Things became clear slowly and painfully. Every grin. Every promise. It seemed like every gesture was planned. The realization hit me hard, and I felt empty.

This truth hurt me deeply. I had put all my faith in her, and now that faith felt heavy. There were always strings attached to her love. It felt more like a trade than care. When I think back on it, a lot of it seems empty. The memories that used to be so important to me now seemed dirty.

Even knowing all of this didn't help the pain go away. It stayed. Every thought she had made the wound worse. I felt like I was being used. Like I had been part of a plan I didn't agree to. And no matter how hard I tried to doubt it, the truth was always there in every memory we shared.

What we had was real to me. It meant the world to me. For her, it was just a way to get what she wanted. That truth hurt more than the betrayal did.

She kept trying for two weeks. Messages. Calls. Every day. "Good morning" in the morning. "Can we talk?" at night. Calls that came in late at night. Her name kept coming up on my screen. Then, all of a sudden, it stopped. No phone calls. No messages. Nothing but silence.

At first, the silence was a relief. But it quickly turned into a different kind of pain. It hurt that she wasn't there. It seemed like the end. Like she had given up. And in doing so, she took a piece of me with her.

I still couldn't get away.

I was tied up without any ropes.

Stuck inside walls made of emotions.

The quiet made me feel heavy. Too heavy and hard to breathe. I started to wonder if this was really the end. Did she already move on? Was I just a memory to her now? The idea hurt a lot. A dull pain settled in my chest and wouldn't go away.

As time went on, the truth sank in more. I felt alone. Left behind at the end of it all. The person who used to mean everything to me was now just a memory. It hurt that she wasn't there. Her voice, her touch, and even her attempts to reach me made the pain worse. It felt like the wound was opening up again and again. A reminder that she might not have ever been mine.

I pictured her living her life as if I had never been there. Going forward without thinking twice. That thought hurt more than the betrayal itself. The hardest thing was realizing that she no longer cared about me. That I was just another chapter that she had finished. It was like everything we had was erased, and there was nothing left.

Even though I didn't answer her calls or texts, I still wanted what we used to have. Every little thing she did to try to reach out kept a weak hope alive. There might still be something there. Something that needs to be saved. A thin thread that hurt, but I couldn't bring myself to cut it.

It felt like the ground gave way beneath me when the calls stopped, and the messages stopped coming. That little bit of hope I had was gone. The truth became clear. She had moved on. The silence that came after felt louder than anything we had ever said. It had a sense of finality that I wasn't ready for.

It wasn't just that she wasn't there that hurt. I realized I had been holding on to a false hope. The hope that once kept me going now seemed cruel. It was like waiting for something that would never happen. I had been standing in the rain, waiting for a storm that had already come and gone.

It wasn't just about losing her. It was about losing the future I had thought about. The version of us that I thought was real. I couldn't lie to myself anymore as the quiet days went on. The bond we had was broken beyond repair. Memories that used to make me feel better now hurt. Touching it hurts.

There was a time when little things made me happy. Walking without a plan. Seeing life go by around me. Thinking about where the road would take me. Everything felt empty without Nadi now. The world seemed boring. Less noise. It looked like it had lost its colour because she wasn't there. The streets we used to walk together didn't feel like home anymore. The places we shared felt like they were haunted.

I still couldn't let myself go.

I was tied up without chains.

Stuck inside walls made of emotions.

It made me think of war. You realize how easy it was to start a war than to end. It was easy to fall for Nadi. It felt like I couldn't let go. I had already lost before I knew I was fighting. The fight was over, but the wounds stayed.

My phone rang one day while I was busy working. It was the desk at the front.

They said, "A guest is waiting for you."

I didn't give it much thought. Even though I had finished what I was doing, I still had work on my mind when I went to the waiting area.

When I walked in, I felt a strange sense of unease. The woman who was sitting there got up. The veil covered her face but not her eyes. Those eyes. Known. Far away. They met mine, and everything else went away.

I recognized those eyes.

I said the name before I could stop myself.

"Nadi…"

For a short time, I couldn't move. She quickly looked away, as if she couldn't stand to look at me. Her eyes went up for a second and then back down.

She looked like she was restless. She fidgeted with her hands, trying to calm down but failing. She stood still, quiet, and almost fragile. Something always got in the way when she tried to look at me. The silence between us was heavy. Like a wall that you can't see.

The sun hit her skin, and I saw the little mole under her lip. She never looked me in the eye.

"I wanted to come to you," she said, "but I couldn't. You know that going out of the club is hard for me. And I didn't know where you lived. I found your visiting card in my purse out of the blue yesterday."

She stopped and waited.

"I kept praying that I would find you here."

I didn't say anything.

She took a breath and held on to her scarf. "Please, say something. Yell at me. Please ask me anything, but don't be quiet. Your silence is hurting me."

Her voice shook. Her hand was on mine, unsure and shaking. There was a lot of feeling in her eyes. Asking for something I wasn't sure I could give.

There was a lot of tension between us. Full of all the things we had never worked out. My heart felt weak, like it was about to break. It was about to break because she was there.

Finally, I spoke, and my voice was low and heavy.

"Nadi, do you know what hurts me the most? I can't look at you the same way I used to. It might have been a game for you. It was my heart."

Something inside her broke. I saw it happen. Her hands shook. She couldn't breathe. She tried to stop the tears from coming, but they came anyway. She opened her mouth, but nothing came out. She stood there in silence, holding on to her dress tightly.

The distance between us felt like it was killing me. I could see her pain clearly. But I couldn't get in touch. I couldn't make her feel better.

For a moment, she was quiet, then she took a deep breath.

"I never meant to hurt you," she said. Her voice was shaking.

"Oh, really? I spoke. "You raised me up to the sky only to let me fall. I'm lying on the ground right now, broken. I don't even know where the parts are. I still need to look for them. And you did all of this for money?"

I shook as I spoke.

She looked me straight in the eye. "Do you think I did it for money?"

"What else?" I asked.

Her eyes filled up, but she fought hard not to cry. One tear fell and slowly rolled down her cheek, stopping near the little mole on her lip. She blinked to hold back the rest. But once the first tear fell, the rest of them did too. One after the other. Like the rain. She tried not to pay attention to them.

She let go of my hand. The one she had been holding for a long time. Then she wiped her face with the back of her hand, like a kid trying to hide their sadness. I quietly took out a box of tissues and put it in front of her.

I thought, "Silly woman, do you even know what this one tear means to me? I would have given everything I had for it."

Nadi was always on top of things and calm. I wasn't ready to see her like this. It seemed like the strong woman I knew was gone, and now there was someone who was weak and vulnerable. She took a tissue and gently wiped her eyes.

When she finally calmed down, she looked up and said in a soft voice,

"I didn't come here to change your mind. I only wanted to see you one last time."

I asked, "Why now?" without thinking.

She glanced at me quickly. "At first, you didn't know why you came to me, today I don't know the answer."

I couldn't get her words out of my head. After a pause, she asked something I wasn't ready for.

"Can I see the ocean?"

I nodded and took her to the window. For a long time, we stood there without saying anything. She stared at the horizon, lost in her own thoughts. I stood next to her and didn't say anything. The ocean went on and on in front of me. The waves crashed in a way that felt too familiar.

Then she asked gently, without looking at me,

"Can I stay here a little longer?"

I thought about it for a second before saying, "Of course."

She kept looking at the ocean and spoke softly, her voice full of regret.

"We only look at the top of the ocean. The waves. And then decide how pretty it is. But we don't know what's inside. How much dark it has. How much violence and innocence can live together?

She stopped for a moment, then went on.

"I wanted to keep you from pain and worry, no matter what happened between us. But in the end, I was the cause of it."

She stopped again and thought about what to say.

"My heart told me to leave you. Not to mess with you. I thought you were different when I first saw you. But something changed when I saw you again."

Her voice got softer.

"I don't know when you first knew you loved me. It began for me that very day. I always thought about you. So much that it made me angry at times."

She finally looked at me. She had sad eyes.

"I tried to stay away from you and to keep you away from me," she said. "But the more I tried, the more I felt like I was getting closer to you."

I didn't answer; instead, I asked, "Do you want to go now or stay a little longer?"

"Let's go," she said.

We walked back to my office this time. I got her a chair and sat down next to her. It felt like the distance between us was both small and impossible.

Her fingers lightly tapped on the armrest. A habit that makes you nervous. We didn't say anything.

I then quietly asked, "Do you want tea or coffee?"

She said, "Coffee."

I did it. When I gave her the cup, our fingers touched for a second.

I said carefully, "Nadi." "Can I say something?"

She nodded. "Yes."

"You make life feel beautiful every time I see you. I can't put into words how beautiful you are. But it's not just what you did that hurts. It's because you did it."

I swallowed and went on.

"You couldn't keep your word. I only asked for one thing. And you wouldn't even look at me like I didn't exist as I was not relevant."

She didn't say anything while she listened.

After that, she asked, "Can I talk?"

"I'm sorry," she said, "but you can't judge without knowing why."

"Really? Am I judging? I spoke.

"Yes," she said in a calm voice. "You don't know my world. That was just a moment at the club. Not the reasons why it happened"

I took a breath and tried to keep myself together.

"I know you have to dance."

"I know you have to talk to others."

"I know where girls from the club go when they're done working, where they spend nights."

My voice got a little louder.

"You Know? when my dad told me to leave my mom, she didn't stop him. I hated her when I saw her laughing with him later but I accepted this with all these things"

I stopped for a moment and then said softly,

"I wanted you more than anything else in life. I found peace with you."

I couldn't say anything else.

She turned away and then looked back at me.

"You want Nadi," she said, "but not the real me. Still now, you want the one you thought of."

I said, "Nadi, please." "Stop playing games."

She sighed. Her shoulders dropping a bit. Like the weight of her words was too much to carry. " I never played any games with you, and I didn't use any tactic either. Everything I did, I did to keep you away from yourself, and me away from you. Playing games with you wasn't hard then, and it isn't hard now. You haven't seen the basic games girls like us play, honestly, I could still play games with you. You wouldn't even notice, and it wouldn't be hard for me"

Her voice dropped almost to a whisper. "But today I'm here to tell you the truth. I'm not here to play games."

Her words threw me into a storm of emotions I could no longer control. The room felt smaller. The air heavier. Like her confession had shifted something basic between us.

Her voice was quiet but sharp. "You say you feel empty inside. Like nothing affects you. Do you know why that is?"

I didn't want to, but her words caught my attention. And a flicker of something I couldn't ignore began to stir inside me.

She continued. Her tone calm but with an intensity that demanded my focus. "When we love someone, when we seek their attention, when we want them, who's the one feeling that need? It's us. It's our want. So, if it's our own need, why do we expect something in return?"

Her words hung in the air. Rich with meaning. She leaned slightly forward. Looking directly into my soul. Like she could see right through me.

"Love is about giving. About sacrificing. About letting go. It's not about getting something back."

She asked, "You stopped loving your mother because she seemed happier with your father. Why did you feel that way? You don't actually know how to love. You just want to be loved." Her eyes softened briefly, but the weight of her words only grew heavier.

She lowered her voice, but the intensity of her words filled the room. Wrapping around us like a storm. "The truth is we don't truly understand love. We confuse it with so many other things. Our wants. Our wishes. Even lust. When we say we love someone, what we're really doing is trying to fill our needs. It starts with wanting. Needing someone or something to fill our emotional gaps. That 'want' is what we call love, but it's not. It's something else entirely."

Her voice was calm, but the truth behind her words felt like a mirror held up to my soul. Reflecting things, I'd never wanted to see. The walls of the office seemed to close in as she spoke.

"What we think is love is often just our own wants and needs dressed up as something deeper. It's not about the other person. It's about filling a void inside ourselves. When we say we love someone, we're really just chasing our own needs and calling them love for someone else."

She paused. Her eyes steady but softened by something I couldn't quite name. Regret maybe. Or a deep sadness. "Today I'm not here for you, but for myself."

"And I love you. My feelings are real, and I don't expect anything from you in return. Your identity. Your actions. They're no longer my concern. All I care about is loving you." Her voice dropped to almost a whisper.

She stood up from her chair. Her movements careful but graceful. Like every step carried the weight of her confession. Her gaze met mine with a sudden intensity. Showing a raw, unfiltered emotion, I'd never seen before. For a moment she closed her eyes. Like she was gathering her thoughts or steadying her resolve.

In the silence I could hear the faint rhythm of her breathing. Steady yet quickened. Echoing the unspoken words that hung between us. She stepped closer. Her presence overwhelming. My heart raced, and without thinking I closed my eyes.

Her lips brushed my cheek in a kiss so gentle it felt like a whisper. Followed by the soft touch of her fingers grazing my lower lip. It was brief, yet it stayed in the air like a question left unanswered. As she pulled away, I opened my eyes to find her already seated back in her chair. Her gaze turned away. Her expression unreadable.

Finally, I found my voice. Though it came out full of mistrust and curiosity. A storm of emotions and questions swirling inside me. "Is this your basic tactic, the one you use?"

She didn't give a straight answer. She looked at me and tilted her head a little.

"Of all the places you've been, the mountains, forests, streams, and valleys, which one was the most beautiful?"

My thoughts went through memories without my permission. Then it stopped. The first time we went out together. She was in the middle of the trees. Soft light on her face. Relaxed. True. Without meaning to, my eyes went to the small mole under her lip. She saw. I could tell she did.

She asked me another question before I could answer.

"Tell me about the saddest thing you've ever seen."

Then she answered it on her own.

"The saddest thing for me is seeing someone whose life has broken them. Someone who stops trying to make their dreams come true and just lets things happen."

Her words weren't very dramatic. They were calm. I could tell she was talking about herself. Not the strong woman she showed the world, but the one who was hurting inside.

She kept talking, her voice shaking.

"That day at the café was the saddest thing I've ever seen. Do you know why?"

She stopped for a moment and took a deep breath.

"You didn't look at me the same way. It was my fault. And the person who fell apart was the one I was scared to really care about."

Finally, I whispered, "Why are you telling me this now?"

"I don't want your forgiveness," she said. "I just want look at me as you used to. When you look at me, I only feel seen"

She looked at her hands.

"We talk about love a lot, but do we ever think about where it comes from? Who makes it?"

I stayed still. Letting her words sink in.

She said, "If a woman doesn't have love in her heart, then love doesn't exist. Money can't buy it. Money can't make it happen. You can't trade love."

She looked me right in the eye to make sure I understood.

"A man can have a woman next to him and still not love her. This is a common mistake for men. They think that buying things means getting love."

She ran her fingers along the edge of the table.

"When a man looks for love, he hopes a woman will make him feel whole again. But money and gestures don't make love. It comes from respect. Because of how you treat her. From being patient and understanding."

She spoke in a lower voice.

"You can't buy love. You can only let it grow. And if it's not there, nothing can make it happen."

She turned her head away for a second.

"So, the question isn't how to get a woman. It's how to earn her love."

She stopped for a moment before continuing.

"When I first saw you at the club, you looked different. You didn't look like you wanted to have sex. But when I heard you call for me at the café, I started to see you like everyone else. I didn't believe you."

Her voice got softer.

"When I walked into that café and saw you stand up for me, I was shocked. No one had ever done that before. That little thing you did when I left, and you stood again, meant the world to me."

She took a deep breath.

"I was with you for a long time and never felt unsafe. You didn't push. You didn't make anyone do anything. You let my walls fall down by themselves. You made me feel like a person. Not wanted for anything. Just seen."

She stopped.

"If a woman like me can fall in love, it's because of who she is. Nothing else."

Then she said in a low voice,

"I couldn't keep my word. Sorry about that."

I asked, "How can you act like you love someone when you don't? Why do this?"

She stared at me for a long time before smiling sadly.

"Do you think a man who hugs us really loves us?"

She shook her head.

"Everything here is fake."

She took a big breath.

"It's time for me to go."

I wanted to tell her to stay. The words almost got away from me. But I ate them.

I told her, "You can go whenever you want."

She smiled as if she knew what was going on.

Then she said, "Can I ask you something?"

I remained silent.

She said, "I want to walk with you one last time. On that same sidewalk, Under the same trees."

I didn't say anything. She stood up, fixed her veil, and said,

"I'll be waiting for you tomorrow night."

She went away. I went with her to the elevator without saying a word.

Her words stayed after she left. Taking apart everything I thought I knew about love. I believed my love was real. Not selfish. But it wasn't. Instead of accepting her for who she was, I was trying to make her into what I thought was perfect.

Was that love?

I saw what was real. My love was about having power. About need. About putting something inside of me.

I could see her clearly for the first time. With no expectations. No conditions. And only then did I know what love really was.

After that, time went by slowly. I couldn't concentrate. I got out of work early. Went home. Put on different clothes. Tried to calm my mind.

There was one feeling waiting quietly under the chaos.

I wanted to meet her again.

I got there fifteen minutes early and was surprised to see her already there. Her face lit up when she saw me. Just pure joy. She had on the same jeans, kurta, and small dupatta around her neck. She knew I liked the outfit. It was a quiet choice, but it said a lot.

"Hi," she said in a soft voice. Then she said, "I knew you'd come. Thanks for coming."

I smiled back. My chest was full. Words didn't seem to matter because I was so full. At that moment, I knew how much I loved her. Not in a way that needed to be explained. It was just something that was there. It's too big to explain. Like trying to hold the ocean in your hands.

This love had nothing to do with wanting or expecting anything. It was just being there. Being aware of her presence. That was all it took.

As she started to walk, I walked next to her without thinking. She took us to the park. The path was surrounded by tall trees, and the light and shadow changed around us. The air was chilly. It smelled like dirt and leaves. The world slowly faded away.

We didn't say anything. There was something in the silence. The leaves made noise. There was a low hum of traffic in the distance. Every step felt like it was carefully planned. It felt like we both knew how fragile this moment was.

She stopped under the trees. Stood still. She looked ahead as if she were looking for something only, she could see. The light touched her face softly. That little mole under her lip caught my eye again. Time seemed to stop. Like the moment wanted to be remembered.

When she looked at me, I was lost in thought.

She kept walking without saying a word. Then she said something. Her voice was steady, but it was heavy.

"Nadi," I said softly.

She didn't say anything.

I said "Nadi" again, this time louder.

Nothing yet. Just the steps she took to move forward.

I stopped and yelled, "Nadi!"

She smiled and turned back.

She didn't say anything, but her smile said everything. She heard me every time. She was waiting. Waiting for me to say her name the way I really meant it.

She said softly, "You've been looking for something real." "But you've been looking in the wrong places."

Her words made me slow down.

"You're looking for approval." Trying to fill a hole inside you. You let people in just because they showed you what you thought you needed.

Her words hit home. Touching things I had been avoiding for a long time.

"You have a rare beauty inside you," she said again. "Your care. Your respect. That's what made me love you. I knew how much it would cost me. I was aware of the risks I was taking. But I still picked it. The life I used to have is over. I don't know what will happen next."

She looked like a butterfly to me. As she walked, the ground barely touched her feet. I realized that the weight I carried had always been mine as I watched her.

She was more than what I had imagined her to be. And this was love. Letting someone be who they are.

I said, "I found reality through you."

"You were looking for it," she said.

"Why did I act that way?" I asked.

She said softly, "You think differently. People like you don't just want to own things. You need to surrender. Without surrender, love can't be felt."

She kept going softly.

"We put up walls. Then we look for love without seeing those walls."

"Don't chase after love. It's something to let happen."

I felt something inside me let go.

I said, "Maybe we just need to let go."

She shook her head.

"Love means being free. Giving and getting. Not in charge."

I said "Nadi" softly.

For a moment, she shut her eyes. I could feel her shiver. Our fingers touched. She stopped moving. All other things went away.

I said again, "Nadi." This time, completely.

She opened her eyes and stared at me. I couldn't say what she knew, but it seemed like she did.

"I love you," I said.

She smiled softly.

"Words don't do a good job of expressing feelings. These are poor translation of our feelings"

"Exactly," I said.

We kept walking. She took my hand when I let go of it.

"Nadi, can I say something to you?"

"Huh?"

"I've never been jealous from anyone before. But now I do."

She laughed. Really laughed. Clear and bright. It was like seeing something grow. She stopped laughing and smiled quietly.

She said, "Love isn't real without jealousy." "I feel it too." It's not about not believing. It's fear. Fear of losing something valuable."

She gave my hand a little squeeze.

She said softly, "And that fear means love is real."

8

The office was quiet except for the sound of my computer and the occasional rustling of papers. The sharp ring of my phone broke the silence while I was deep in my work and focused. When I looked at the screen, my heart skipped a beat. I saw Nadi's name. Why was she calling at this time? As I spoke, worry grew in my chest.

"Please come to the club today," she said, her voice tense. It shook a little bit. This wasn't like her at all. She didn't sound so upset very often.

"Is everything all right?" I asked, my voice full of worry.

"Yes, everything is fine," she said. Her voice got softer, but the same intensity stayed. "But please come to the club."

I paused, my mind racing with questions. "Okay, I'll be there."

"Thanks," she said. Then, almost like an afterthought, "I love you." The line went dead before I could say anything.

The hours dragged on, and I couldn't concentrate. The sound of her voice. What she said. The shake I heard. I remembered everything. When the time came, I went to the club with my heart racing with excitement and worry. There was a lot going on in the hotel lobby, but I didn't care. I was only thinking about her.

I tried to call her again, but she didn't pick up. The quiet made me more worried. A hotel staff member came up to me just as I was about to give up. They were calm but had a purpose.

They pointed to the elevators and said, "Sir, if you'll follow me."

I followed, even though I was confused. The ride to the top floors seemed to go on forever. Every second made my thoughts more and more tangled with options. The staff member took me to a fancy room with a door that was slightly open, smiled knowingly, and left me alone.

I hesitated because my heart was beating so hard that I thought it could be heard through the door. I stopped when I pushed it open. Nadi was in front of me. Her presence filled the room like a storm that was quiet.

Without saying a word, she stepped forward and hugged me tightly. I held her just as tightly, and my hands shook against her back. Her heart raced against my chest, matching the wild beat of mine. For a short time, the outside world didn't exist. It was only her.

When we finally let go, her hands stayed on my arms, and her grip was strong, as if she was afraid, I would disappear. She looked into my eyes. They were filled with a storm of feelings. Something deeper that I couldn't put a name to. She was saying things that she couldn't say.

She led me to the bed and sat down, moving with grace and confidence while looking at me. I knelt down in front of her, my hands on her knees, and my heart was still racing. The room was quiet, and the air was thick with things that weren't said.

As she got closer, her breath touched my skin. The soft, floral smell of her perfume filled the air around us. I loved the little mole under her lips that she opened up a little bit.

"You said once, this mole is your whole world," she whispered, her voice shaking with hope and fear. "Take your world."

Her words hung in the air between us. I couldn't breathe as I tried to figure out what she was offering.

When I saw her closed eyes, I felt a rush of emotion. In the warm light, her face glowed, and I could feel her pulse racing under her skin, keeping time with mine.

Our noses touched. I could feel her breath on my lips.

I leaned in and kissed the little mole under her lip. Her breathing slowed and became shallow, and she melted into my arms. Her hands wrapped around my neck and pulled me closer, not wanting to let go. She turned her head to the side, showing off the graceful curve of her neck.

There were bangles on her wrists, one green and one red. A few fell off and hit the floor softly while she held on to me. It sounded like music.

I could tell she was losing it. She shook her arms to try to keep herself together. I held her face and kissed her forehead before she could fall onto the bed. She weakly protested, her voice a soft plea. "Don't leave."

What she said hit home. Her eyes, which are usually bright, were dark with feeling. She held on to my shirt with her hands, her face was red, and her breathing was uneven. Her hair fell loosely over her shoulders and caught the light. She had tears in her eyes, but she wouldn't let them fall. She pressed closer, shaking, her mole standing out against her glowing skin. Her neck was bare and open.

She held on to me like I was her only lifeline. I held her steady by wrapping my arms around her.

I said softly, "Nadi.I 'm here. I'm not going anywhere."

She looked at me, looking for something. Then she let go of my hand and put her forehead against mine.

All of a sudden, she put her face in my chest and shook her shoulders with silent sobs. I held her close and stroked her hair.

I said her name over and over again. "Nadi."

Her fingers were stuck to my shirt because she was scared to let go. I lightly brushed her cheek until she made a soft, sleepy sound. At first, she didn't want to open her eyes, and her lashes fluttered, but then she did. I smiled because it felt like the world had become smaller and smaller.

"What happened?" I asked quietly.

She didn't answer; instead, she put her arms around me again and rested her head on my shoulder. We stayed that way, quiet, with my fingers running through her hair and our breathing steady.

After a while, she whispered, "I was in heaven." Then she playfully asked, "Why did you bring me back?" She tapped me on the shoulder lightly.

I smiled. "Nadi, I'm hungry."

"No, just sit still," she said again, tapping me and leaving her hand there.

In that quiet, I felt something warm and definitely hers. The smell of her, the way she was there, something that stuck with me.

She let me go when I finally tried to move. She looked away, and her cheeks were slightly red. I tried to get a cigarette, but she took it from me and the lighter. She fought with it, her brows furrowed, and then she coughed after taking a small puff. She gave it back with a small, proud smile.

I took a drag and watched her lean back against the pillows to make room for me. I put my head on her lap. She slowly and carefully ran her fingers through my hair, and each touch made me feel better. She didn't say anything as she brushed the ash away.

Every move felt like love. Like love.

She put the ashtray away and took the finished cigarette. I turned on my side, and she kept stroking my hair with her soft, soothing fingers. My body let go of all its tension. Her touch was so comforting that my thoughts faded away. As the world outside faded away, all that mattered was the warmth of her lap and the soft touch of her fingers.

I felt it, a soft, lingering kiss on my cheek, as sleep started to pull me under. Her lips were warm, and her breath felt light on my skin. Everything faded away into a peaceful dream where she and I were together.

I woke up to find Nadi's fingers still softly tangled in my hair, but her hand was still. I quietly said her name, hoping she would answer. I called again, my voice barely above a whisper. She didn't say anything back. I couldn't help but smile. She might have wanted me to say her name again. I tried a few more times, but she didn't move. Her breathing was calm and steady, like an anchor in the stillness of the room.

I put my hand over hers and felt her skin against mine. I turned over slowly and looked up at her.

She had her eyes closed. Her face was calm as she slept. I had never seen Nadi asleep before. Her beauty was even more striking because she looked calm. Her steady breathing, like the waves of the sea, made her even more beautiful. The little mole under her lip stood out against her glowing face, making her look perfect. I couldn't stop looking at her. She was the most beautiful thing I had ever seen in that quiet moment. She was a picture of peace and grace that I wanted to keep forever.

I saw her eyes flutter open and she saw that I was awake. She smiled softly and touched my cheek with her fingertips. It was such a light touch that it took my breath away.

"Did you just get up?" She asked in a soft voice, like the first light of dawn. "Why didn't you wake me up too?"

"Yes," I said, calm but firm. "I feel like I've really slept for the first time in my whole life."

She turned to look at me, her eyes reflecting the soft light in the room and her face deep in thought. "We can only see the world through our own eyes, we really don't know much."

"I used to think that sleeping meant lying down, closing your eyes, and falling asleep. But today I learned that real sleep is not the same as just resting, and you showed me that real sleep doesn't even need to be lying down."

"Today I agree with you. We can't really think freely; we just use what we know and have been through."

There was something warm and mysterious in her eyes, like a secret that only she knew. .

Our talk was like a calm stream that brought us closer together. She turned her head and asked softly, "Are you hungry?"

I thought for a second, then shook my head and smiled. "Not anymore."

She leaned in so that her lips brushed my ear. Her eyes sparkled with mischief. "But now... I'm starving," she said, barely above a whisper. I got a chill from what she said, and I didn't want it to go away.

"What do you want to eat?" I asked, my voice weaker than I thought it would be.

"Everything," she said with a hint of mischief in her voice.

I laughed. "Could you be a little clear?"

She thought for a moment and tilted her head. "You once talked about grilled chicken from a place nearby."

I nodded. "I did." I'll get that.

I rested my head in her lap and let her fingers play with my hair while we waited. There was something in the silence between us. It was warm, comforting, and full of understanding that didn't need to be said.

When the food came, Nadi lit a cigarette, took a slow drag, and gave it to me. "Here." While I get things ready, smoke.

I saw her move with grace as she carefully arranged everything. She called me over when it was ready. She didn't give me a plate; instead, she picked up a piece of chicken and held it to my lips.

"Here," she said with a smile. "I want to share my first bite."

I leaned in and tasted not only the food but also the love behind the gesture.

"May I ask you a question?" She said this while we were eating, calm but steady.

I nodded and chewed slowly.

"Why didn't you answer my texts?" You just sat there quietly in the café that day. Why didn't you call me rude or disloyal or dishonest, like most people would have?"

I looked at her, and she looked at me with eyes that were looking for answers. "Should I have?"

She sighed and gave me another piece of chicken. "That's what most people would have done."

"I know," I said, taking my time to chew. "But we often think too much about what we've lost in love instead of what it's given us."

Her eyes were fixed on mine, steady and waiting.

"Yes, I was angry with you. But I had already gotten so much from your love. If it was real or just a trick of the mind. You brought me back to life when I was emotionally numb. So even though I was hurt, it would have been wrong to call you unfaithful or mean. You gave me something that can't be taken away, no matter what."

She asked a question that wasn't real, but she sounded worried. "What would happen if I left right away? Gone without a trace. Would you say I'm unfaithful?"

I looked into her eyes and said honestly, "Don't even say that."

She smiled a little, as if she were imagining different situations. "Just a thought, but would you still think I'm faithful?"

I didn't think twice. "Always. And I'll always love you."

She looked at me with respect. "That's just one of the many things that make you different from anyone else I've met."

After dinner, Nadi led me to the bed and put a pillow behind me so I could sit cross-legged against the headboard, just like she had done before. She put an ashtray next to me, lit a cigarette, and gave it to me. Then she lay on her side with her head in my lap, propped up on one hand, and let me run my fingers through her hair. Suddenly, she grabbed my wrist.

"Don't do that," she said, putting my hand under her cheek instead.

The silence between us was warm and unbroken until her voice shook with the question. "Am I not pretty? Don't you think I'm a woman?"

I could feel the weight of what she said, but I just answered. "Nadi, beauty is a private language." For me, it was always about making an ideal in my mind and loving it. Then you came and broke every picture I had made. You showed me how God is an artist when I couldn't see it. I still think that some people have the power to give life to things that are dead. And for me, that's you."

She didn't say anything. She just pushed my hand harder against her face, as if to seal my truth into her skin.

After that, she turned over and looked at me for a second before patting the space next to her. "Lie down," she said, her voice friendly.

I sat down next to her, and she put her head on my arm. We lay there for a few quiet seconds, her body warm against mine and her breath steady. The room was quiet, and the world outside seemed to disappear, leaving us alone in this silence.

Then she turned to face me, moving slowly and on purpose. Her breathing sped up as she got closer, her lips brushing my earlobe. A shiver ran through me, a spark that made my heart race. She kissed my cheek softly, rubbed her nose against mine, and closed her eyes. Her face was calm, as if she were lost in the moment.

She suddenly moved closer, her lips brushing against mine and then gently biting my lower lip. I turned my head in surprise and offered my neck.

She didn't think twice. Her lips touched the sensitive spot under my ear. Kisses are soft but firm. She moved her hands with purpose; one slid up my chest while the other played with the buttons on my shirt. Her fingers shook a little, but she was determined, as if she were trying to close the gap between us in the only way she knew how.

I could tell she was losing control because her breath was shallow and her body was getting closer.

I couldn't speak clearly, so I whispered, "Nadi."

She only made a soft, questioning sound and kept tracing her lips along my neck.

I tried again, but it was hard to hear. "Nadi... please. No. "Please stop."

But she didn't. Her hands kept searching, soft but desperate. I held her face in my hands and tried to bring her back to me, but her eyes stayed closed and her body didn't respond. She was somewhere far away.

I said "Nadi" again, this time with more force. Please. That's enough. "Stop."

Her eyes opened and met mine with a mix of confusion and defiance. "No?" she asked, her voice shaking.

I looked into her eyes, my heart breaking. "No," I said firmly.

Her eyes were filled with rage. She pushed my hands away and turned onto her side, resting on my chest with her back to me. We stayed that way for a while, the silence full of things we couldn't say.

I tried to run my fingers through her hair, but she angrily pushed my hand away. I tried again, and after a moment of resistance, she let me go on without saying anything.

She leaned closer, so close that her lips almost brushed my ear. I could feel the warmth of her breath as she spoke, barely above a whisper.

"You were the first person who ever said NO to me," she said softly. "And you were the only one I wanted to say Yes to."

"I never wanted anyone else," she continued. "Everything before you were out of necessity, not choice. I wanted to say no to everyone, but I couldn't. And when I finally met the one person I chose with my heart, the one person I never wanted to refuse. I wanted to feel what a bride feels. I've never surrendered to anyone before. My body has slept in other beds, but my heart never closed its eyes. I've been touched, but never held."

She kissed my cheek softly and started to pull back, but I didn't let her go. I held her face in my hands and looked into her eyes until she closed them. I kissed the tiny mole under her lower lip. Then both of her eyelids, gently, like closing something sacred. Finally, I pressed my lips to her forehead, slowly, like a promise.

That's when I felt it: a quiet trembling in her, like a held breath finally released. When I pulled back, she was smiling. Not the bright smile she showed the world, this was smaller, softer. Real.

I drew her head to my shoulder. She leaned into me. And then, with my fingers moving through her hair, slowly, again and again, it felt less like a goodbye and more like… a beginning.

We talked for a long time, and our words and looks were like threads that made us feel close. I looked at my watch every now and then because I knew it was almost time for her to leave.

As the moment drew near, the mood changed and became heavy with unspoken sadness. I could tell by the way she stood and the way she kept looking at me that my refusal had made a distance between us that neither of us knew how to close. The air was charged with feelings that neither of them could put into words. It seemed impossible to say goodbye.

We hugged tightly before she left, not wanting to let go. She hugged me tightly, with her face pressed against my shoulder. It seemed like she was comforting me while holding onto something weak inside of her. She tried to smile, but her eyes were full of tears that sparkled like stars in the dark.

"I'll see you soon," she said, her voice shaking. We didn't know if it was a promise or a wish.

I nodded, my throat tight.

I walked her to the door, my heart heavy. Each step felt like a countdown I wasn't ready for. She stopped at the landing and looked back at me, her eyes full of tears that she wouldn't let fall. Time stopped. It felt like the world was just us.

I smiled at her, and she ran back and hugged me tightly. I held her just as tightly, as if I could keep her there forever. She whispered in my ear, "You look so beautiful when you smile." Keep smiling all the time.

Her words were soft, gentle, and fragile, and they hung in the air like a promise. Then, too soon, she let go. She walked away without looking back. Her hug stayed in the empty space she left behind. There may have been tears she didn't want me to see. She might not have wanted me to see. Maybe she didn't want me to know how hard it was for her to leave.

We said goodbye without saying a word. I smiled to comfort her, even though my heart felt like it was breaking. She smiled back, but her lips were so thin that the smile didn't quite reach her eyes.

Then she turned around and left. Her footsteps echoed softly down the stairs until they were gone. I stood still and watched until she was out of sight. The empty room felt heavy and suffocating.

The room felt empty after she left. The silence was heavy on me. It felt like the air was colder. The walls seemed to stretch, and the room seemed too big, as if her absence had made the world bigger. I was lying on the bed and looking at the ceiling. Nadi took over my mind. Her laughter, her touch, and the tears she wouldn't let fall were all I could think about. Every memory played over and over again, but it hurt too much to reach.

I felt a sharp pain in my chest. Not just being alone, but also being afraid of losing something I didn't fully understand. Every minute that went by without hearing from her felt like an eternity. I grabbed my phone. Fingers hovering over the screen. But I just couldn't bring myself to call. What if she didn't want to hear from me? What if my voice was an annoyance? It was worse than being quiet to think that she hated me.

Instead, I typed, "Thanks for tonight." "For everything." I thought about it for a second before hitting send. Just one tick. Not delivered. My heart sank. It's possible that her phone was dead. She might see it when it is charged. I held on to that small hope and put the device down.

I tossed and turned, and the sheets got all tangled up. The bed was too big and empty. The clock made a loud noise. Every second reminds me of how far apart we are getting. I wanted to hear her voice so I would know she was okay. To know that whatever had happened hadn't broken something that couldn't be fixed. But the phone didn't ring. The screen is dark and doesn't care.

Sleep came slowly and with doubt, and I held on to the hope that she would call before morning. Her voice was a lifeline in the dark. I pictured her reaching out to me, her lips curving into that knowing smile that made everything feel right.

I woke up in the afternoon. The curtains let in a lot of light, which made long shadows across the room. Nadi was the first thing that came to mind. I reached for my phone, but it was blank. I pressed the power button, but nothing happened. The battery is dead. Anger rose. I fumbled around for the charger, plugged it in, and pressed the button again. Time dragged on, and every second was too much.

At last, the screen lit up. I looked at my messages. The one from last night: "Thanks for tonight." "For everything." Still just one tick. Not delivered. My stomach turned. It's possible that her phone was off. It could be that she didn't charge it. I checked the connection when I wasn't online. Made it work quickly. Recharged. Nothing.

I felt a wave of worry come over me. What if she forgot to plug it in? What if she hadn't turned it on? I couldn't stay still. I left the hotel. I couldn't stop thinking. I waited for the time she usually woke up. Minutes felt like hours. Time seemed to make fun of me.

When the time came, there was still no answer. I called her number, but it wouldn't connect. Two more hours went by. Nothing. It was still impossible to reach her number.

I couldn't wait any longer. I counted down the days until the club opened. I arrived an hour early and paced outside, my nerves on edge. When the doors finally opened, I rushed in and looked around. There was no one on stage. Women came and took their seats. But Nadi... she was nowhere to be found.

With my heart racing, I went up to a staff member. "Where is Miss Nadia?" "My voice is tight with need."

The staff member blinked, confused. "Nadia?"

"Yes." I said again, "Miss Nadia," my patience running out.

"Oh, she left," he said, as if it were no big deal.

"She left? I asked, my disbelief growing. "Where?"

He shrugged and said, "Sorry, I don't know."

"How come you don't know?" I yelled, my anger boiling over.

"Sir, all I know is that she left. "Nothing more," he said in a defensive tone.

"I insisted," my voice breaking. "Please, just tell me where she is."

The worker showed me to the manager's office. he Smiled politely and offered tea. I didn't pay attention to it. "Please, tell me where Nadia is," I begged.

The manager sighed and leaned back. "Sir, this is a club. A lot of people come and go. Why are you so worried? There are other beautiful women here who are more than happy to help."

My mind wouldn't let me understand what he said. "Just tell me where she is," I said again. Voice breaking.

He stood up when he lost his patience. "She is gone. How many times do we have to say it? We don't know. Don't ask again. "Drink your tea and go."

I kept checking my phone over and over. On and off. Messages that make you feel good. Wishing that the one tick would turn into two. It never did. My message was "Thanks for tonight." "For everything" never got to her, a silent sign of her absence.

I called her number over and over. Every time I called, I got an automated voice saying "unreachable." Chilly. Mechanical. Nothing took away the pain in my chest.

Every time I got a notification, my heart raced because I thought it was her. But it never was. Updates that don't mean anything. Every alert made the emptiness worse. I looked at the screen, hoping it would ring and show her name. No sound.

I couldn't stop moving. I needed to find her. Every club in the city turned into a search, fuelled by a small amount of hope. Rooms with low light, eyes scanning the stages, tables, and performers' faces. Nadi was nowhere to be found. Each club felt less full than the one before it. The music is too loud. The lights are too bright. Grating laughter.

I asked everyone I could think of. Employees, managers, and even performers. "Have you seen Nadi? "Do you know where she is?" Always the same answers: "No, sorry." We don't know her, or worse, "She's gone."

9

The days all ran together. I became more and more frantic and desperate in my search. I went to shady clubs in the city's forgotten corners where I'd never been before, hoping she would be there. But no one had seen her. Nobody knew where she was.

I felt like I was following a ghost. A shadow that always slipped through my fingers when I thought I was close. The more I looked, the more I realized how little I knew about her. I didn't know her full name, where she lived, or who her friends were. All I had were memories of her smile, her voice, and the way she looked at me. I also felt the heavy weight of her absence.

Weeks went by, and there was still no sign of her. I started to wonder if she was real or just a dream that went away with the morning light. But the pain in my chest said otherwise. She was real. And then she was gone.

Without her, I walked the same paths we had walked together, hoping to hear her laughter again. I walked around the streets where we had walked together. The sidewalks seemed less busy. Without her, the city is quieter. I would sometimes stop by the café where we had talked for hours. The smell of coffee and pastries brought back memories of her smile across the table. I would sit by the window where we always did and gaze at the vacant chair opposite me. I half expected her to show up, slide into it with her usual grace, and say, "I'm here." But she never did.

The café used to be a warm place, but now it felt empty, like a shell of what it had been with her. But I kept going back, hoping that being there would somehow bring her closer and close the gap between the past and the present. A hope that was useless, but I couldn't let go of it. Letting go would mean accepting that she was really gone.

Nadi was in my heart. A part of me that would never go away. I couldn't help but smile each time I thought of her, her laughter, her smile, and the way she gazed at me. Those memories pierced the clouds, radiating warmth from within. But occasionally, her memory became a mountain that was so heavy that I could hardly breathe. The anguish of her absence would surge and subside, engulfing me. She was both my happiness and my sadness, my light and my dark. Even though she was gone, she was still with me. She was a quiet presence I carried with me everywhere, like a song I couldn't stop humming, even when it hurt.

While I was fixing my tie, my phone rang. No number is known.

"Hey?"

"Do you remember Nadia?"

Everything came to a stop.

"Yes," I said. "I remember her."

"She's in the hospital. She can't wait to see you."

My screen showed an address. A hospital.

"I'm on my way."

I took my suitcase and ran. The conference, my job, and the life I had built didn't matter. Nadi was the only thing that mattered.

I didn't go to the meeting. Made a reservation for the earliest flight. Her country was hours away, but I didn't think twice.

My office called me at the airport.

"Where are you?" The conference is about to begin.

"Go ahead without me."

I got off the phone, turned it off, and got on the plane.

The flight went by in a flash. I could see her face in every cloud that passed below me. I could hear her laugh and see how she tucked her hair behind her ear. What if I'm too late?

I ran through the airport when I got there. The smell of antiseptic from the hospital mixed with something sour. The walls were cracked, and the floors were scuffed. I didn't care. I just had to find her.

I looked in bed after bed. Then I got the feeling that someone was watching me.

I turned around.

There was a woman. Under the bright fluorescent lights, tears ran down her face.

It was Nadi.

"Nadi?" I said it softly.

She smiled through her tears, and tried to make room for me on the bed.

I ran to her. She didn't look the same. She had hollow cheeks and skin that was almost see-through. But those eyes still had that spark.

I held her hand. So thin. She had bruises and needle marks on her skin. Touching it feels cold.

I said, "Nadi."

She smiled. Not strong, but real.

The mole under her lip was very noticeable on her pale skin. Her hair was thinner and duller now, but she was still Nadi.

She had trouble holding my hand. I wrapped both of mine around hers to try to give her my warmth. She barely squeezed back.

Her hands shook as she raised them to wipe my tears with her scarf. She touched me softly. She never took her eyes off mine.

Then she raised her arms to me. She didn't say anything. She didn't have to.

I leaned in and put my head on her chest. I could hear her heartbeat in my ear. It was weak and steady.

She was still here, with me.

Her hug was weak but strong. The hospital soap couldn't mask the faint smell of her old perfume. The clock stopped. The world outside faded away. Only us.

I wanted to stay there forever. But her breathing was shallow and her grip was weak. I tried to pull away.

She held on more tightly.

"Just a little longer, please," she said softly.

So, I stayed. I could feel her heart beating against my ear. The warmth of her body against mine. Her love, strong and unbreakable, was all around me.

Finally, her grip got looser. She started to breathe more slowly. I looked up at her.

There was love in her eyes.

She said, "You were always on my mind and in my heart." "At first, I would rather not tell you anything. But then I realized you had a right to know. At least then, your heart could be at peace.

She stopped for a moment. "That night, the last time we saw each other, I came to tell you something. I didn't think I was the best person for you. "You deserved better."

The words hurt.

"You came into my life as a guest, but I fell deeply in love with you," she said. "There were so many times when your selflessness shocked me. And then one night, even though I begged you to stay, you turned away from me. I didn't get it at first. But by morning, I knew that all I had been thinking about was your love.

Her voice became softer. "I trust that you'll always be there for me when I need you." I don't know how to really say I apologize for everything, but please forgive me.

I sat there. The medical equipment made a humming sound. People were talking in the distance.

I said, "Nadi, your leaving made me sorrowful, but your love made me very happy." "Why did you leave without saying goodbye?" You left me all by myself.

She stared at me. Sleepy. Tender.

"You look tired and hungry." First, eat something and rest. Later, I'll tell you everything.

I came back after forty-five minutes. She had trouble with some fruit, watched me eat, and then reached out to touch my hair.

I asked, "Are you all by yourself?"

"My mom is busy all day. She comes in the morning and at night.

The door swung open. A woman in her 60s came in with food and fruit. She stopped when she saw me. First there was surprise, then recognition.

Nadi confirmed my identity. The woman came up and smiled. I was standing, but she told me to sit down.

Nadi said, "This is my mother."

Her mother looked at Nadi's face, where there was a faint glow.

She said, "I haven't seen her smile like this in months."

We had a conversation. I learned something from her mother that I didn't know.

"I kept telling her to get in touch with you. For a whole month, she said no before finally saying yes.

The sun went down. Nadi's mother stayed with her, smoothing her hair and moving her blanket. The golden light made Nadi look almost like a light.

Then Nadi said in a low voice, "Can you go home tonight?"

Her mother smiled and nodded. "Yes." She pushed Nadi's hair back and left.

The room got quiet. I sat next to Nadi's bed and kept an eye on her. My eyes were getting heavy, but I fought sleep. Every second counted.

Nadi saw. She moved slowly.

"Come here and lie down next to me."

I wasn't sure what to do.

"Come," she said again.

I slid onto the bed next to her. The area was small. We fit together just like we always had.

"Put your arm under my head," she said softly.

I did. Her hair felt thin on my skin. As she leaned against me, her body shook a little.

We were quiet. Her breathing created a rhythmic pattern. She stared at the ceiling with her eyes. Thinking. Thinking about it.

She found my hand. Our fingers were linked. She squeezed. I squeezed back, being careful not to hurt her.

The world outside disappeared.

Her breaths got shorter. She let go of her grip. But I stayed strong.

She looked away. Looked me in the eye. We communicated a great deal without using any words.

I kissed her on the forehead. "I'm here, Nadi." I'm not leaving.

She shut her eyes. Gave a faint smile. For a moment, she was the old Nadi, the one who made my life better.

But I knew what was true. We had nothing else left.

She ran her fingers through my hair. I closed my eyes and let her touch me to calm me down.

She looked up at the ceiling. "We worry and fear so much, but eventually, we realize that living is what matters most. Living is more important than all those worries.

She couldn't breathe.

"I don't want to die." "I want to live."

I couldn't say anything.

I had an idea later on. I helped her sit up by putting pillows behind her. She looked at me with interest.

I put bangles on her wrists. They made a soft sound.

"I've never seen your hands without bangles on them before," I said. "But today they were bare, so I made sure to get some while I was out getting food."

She ran her fingers over the bangles. She smiled, even though her eyes were full of tears. She held me close with her arms around me. The bangles made a noise between us.

She pulled back after a while and kissed me on the eyes. Her lips were warm.

"I wish I hadn't left you," she said.

I said, "It doesn't matter." "Because every second I spend with you is special to me."

She cried. "What kind of life is this?" I wanted to die, but I kept living. Even though I'm dying, I now want to live. I could have died at any time for any reason. Death is now telling me, "I'm coming soon." I plead with death, saying, "I want to live," but it simply responds, "No, you have only a few days left... get ready."

I held her head in my arms while we lay together. She looked at me. I was already looking at her.

We looked at each other. We could see everything: love, regret, longing, and understanding.

She said, "You were right. Some paths are more beautiful than destinations.

She took a pause and whispered "I love you."

I felt a rush of warmth.

"I love you too," I also whispered.

She put her head on my chest and rested for a while. "Having sex without love is like rape and always hurts, but not letting someone you love have sex is even worse."

I got it. I had nothing to say. I pulled her close and shut my eyes.

It was morning. Sunlight came through the window and danced on Nadi's face.

I heard a noise that woke me up. Nadi's mom was crying. Soft sobs. She put her hands over her mouth and shook her shoulders.

I turned to Nadi. In the morning light, her face looked calm. Bangles caught the sun and made a soft sound.

At first, I was confused because I was still sleepy.

She wasn't moving. Doctors approached the bed, and when confirmed, I got it.

My dear Nadi was gone.

"Nadi, please..." "I can't believe you left me like this," I said. "There were so many things that weren't said and so many dreams that weren't realized."

Her mother lightly touched my shoulder and put Nadi's dupatta in my hand. The cloth was soft. Known.

The room was filled with morning light, but the world had never felt darker.

I kissed her forehead. One last time. For a short time, I thought she was still with me. It seemed like her weak smile was a message. That she was at peace.

I lost her. But I also felt love. Deep. Fierce. Forever. A love that is stronger than death.

When it was time to bury Nadi, her mother came up to me. Nadi's last wish was for me to spread soil over her grave.

I got it. This was the last thing I did out of love.

I cried a lot. As I spread the soil over Nadi's grave, I let out a long cry. It felt like I was giving up a part of myself with every handful.

The ground felt cool, wet, and heavy in my hands. I felt like it was all over when it fell on her grave.

She was no longer there. But she would always be there for me.

People came together, gravediggers, others, and people who were curious.

They wanted to know who I was and why I was crying.

"I am burying my heart with my hands," I said.

They stared with no expression. They didn't get it.

I turned around and left. No one would ever be able to get back into this heart. After her, nothing would ever feel beautiful to my heart again.

I let my heart rest with Nadi's, hoping that I would soon meet.

www.ingramcontent.com/pod-product-compliance
Lightning Source LLC
Chambersburg PA
CBHW051240130726
47988CB00001B/435